Boogers from Beyond

by M. D. Payne

Grosset & Dunlap
An Imprint of Penguin Group (USA) LLC

To Ben, whose support
is strong as llama spit

GROSSET & DUNLAP
Published by the Penguin Group
Penguin Group (USA) LLC, 375 Hudson Street, New York, New York 10014, USA

USA | Canada | UK | Ireland | Australia | New Zealand | India | South Africa | China

penguin.com
A Penguin Random House Company

Text copyright © 2014 by M. D. Payne. Illustrations copyright © 2014 by Amanda Dockery. All rights reserved.
Published by Grosset & Dunlap, a division of Penguin Young Readers Group, 345 Hudson Street, New York,
New York 10014. GROSSET & DUNLAP is a trademark of Penguin Group (USA) LLC. Printed in the USA.

Cover illustrated by Amanda Dockery

Library of Congress Cataloging-in-Publication Data is available.

ISBN 978-0-448-46228-8   10 9 8 7 6 5 4 3 2 1

Prologue

The old monster quivered with fear.

"Thank . . . uh, thank . . . you for seeing me," it stammered while bowing low.

A dark, hooded figure slowly approached the old monster. His long, shimmering cape extended past his feet, and he appeared to be floating a few feet off of the ground. In his long arms he held a purring cat. The figure stroked the cat with gloved hands.

A hiss-like voice came from within the dark hood. "You've come a long way. I hope for your sake that the journey was worth it. Speak. But prove to me why I should listen."

From somewhere deep underground, a massive

roar shook the ancient throne room. White dust from the high ceiling slowly rained down on them, causing the cat to hiss.

"There, there," said the figure soothingly to the cat. "You'll feast soon."

The old monster brushed the dust off of his shoulders, trying to fight through his fear. "I can get you into their new facility," he said. "I can give you all of them."

"You offer me nothing. I've already weakened their defenses," said the floating figure. His eyes glowed from somewhere deep in the hood. The cat hissed in agreement as its eyes, too, began to glow. "Their old facility has been destroyed. Their spirits have been crushed—they will be easy to pick off. I have already won. Those old monsters just haven't realized it yet. As for you, I will have you drained of every last drop of lebensplasm for wasting our time."

The cat hissed at the monster as the hooded figure motioned to two guards who had appeared at the door. The figure floated up toward a massive hole in the stone ceiling. The cat growled ominously as they rose.

The guards, cloaked in red, moved toward the old monster.

"No, wait!" screeched the old monster as he fell to his knees. "They're stronger than you think. They're the strongest ones left, thanks to Paradise Island. The

Director has chosen a new, secure facility. You'll never be able to defeat him without my help."

The hooded figure ignored the monster's pleas.

"And you'll never find his *pendants* without me," added the monster.

The hooded figure paused his rise and extended his hand. The cloaked guards immediately halted their advance.

"Did you say 'pendants'? That fool has more than one?!" howled the hooded figure.

The old monster rose to his feet as the guards backed away.

"You have my attention," the hooded figure said as he hovered just above the ground. "Now tell me *everything* you know about the location of these pendants."

"He has one piece that he wears around his neck," the old monster replied confidently. "And the other he keeps hidden. I can find it and bring them both to you."

"And what do you ask for in return?" asked the hooded figure.

"I'm sick of being eternally old," said the old monster. "I'm sick of being weak. And I know how this all is going to end. If I don't do something now, you'll just drain me like all the rest. I need you to promise you won't harm me."

"Very well," said the hooded figure, "you have my word. You shall be considered one of us. Now, I have—"

"Wait," the old monster cut him off. "It's not just about me. There's something more I need you to do."

"SOMETHING MORE?" the voice hissed from deep within the hood. "You dare to ask me for more than your pitiful soul? What more could you want?"

"My sister," choked the old monster, holding back tears. "I need you to bring my sister back. You can do that, can't you?"

"Yes, but why should I?" hissed the hooded figure. "This talk of family disgusts me."

"I would rather die right now, at this very spot, than keep on without her," said the old monster. "But I'm much more useful to you alive, am I not?"

"For the time being," said the hooded figure. "But don't dare to disappoint me. There are fates worse than being drained of your energies until you gasp your last breath, I can assure you.

"I don't trust you to do this alone," the figure added as he dropped the cat onto the floor.

He clapped his hands, and the two guards once again stood at attention. "Bring me Test Subject Q," demanded the hooded figure.

"Q?" asked one guard. "But, Master, I thought you had deemed Q unworthy."

"Did I ask you to think?" threatened the hooded figure. "If I wanted you to think, I'd have you working in the lab—now bring me Test Subject Q!"

The guard left and returned a short time later with a huge woolly monster with terrible fangs—like a mutated buffalo mixed with an abominable snowman. He held it with a glowing leash that crackled as the monster rose and swiped its huge paws in the air.

"Let it loose," said the hooded figure.

"Master?!" the guards yelled.

"DO IT!"

The old monster watched, horrified, as they let the beast loose, and it immediately turned on them. It grabbed the closest guard. There was a screech as it shoved its furry face into the guard's hood.

CRUNCH.

"Oh, wonderful." The black hooded figure chuckled and clapped his gloved hands.

"Is this the creature you want me to use?" the old monster asked. "I'll never be able to control it!"

The woolly monster, finished with the guard, turned to the old monster and the hooded figure. It galloped at them.

"No," said the hooded figure over the roar of the terrible woolly creature. "This is."

He pointed at the cat, which took off for the advancing monster.

The monster stopped in its tracks, shrieked in terror, and turned around.

The cat chased it out of the huge doorway, and the

old monster could hear a terrible struggle, the sound of splashing and hissing, tearing flesh, screaming, and then utter silence.

The cat quietly padded its way into the room and licked a bit of blood off of its muzzle.

"I give you . . . the SANGALA!" said the hooded figure. "THIS is the tool that you shall unleash upon the unsuspecting. THIS is the tool that shall tear you to shreds if you dare disappoint me."

Once again, the eyes of the cat glowed ominously like the eyes of the hooded figure. The old monster was very afraid.

"Now, bow down!" The hooded figure's voice boomed throughout the room.

The old monster bowed down and slowly backed out of the massive chamber.

In the Beginning . . .

"All right, smell test," said Shane. He had created a three-point test for Lunch Lady's cafeteria food.

We all leaned in and began to sniff.

"I think I'm good," said Ben. "It doesn't make me feel sick or anything."

He sneezed.

"But you *are* sick," said Gordon. "Can you smell anything but your own boogers?" He leaned in and took another mega-whiff of his food.

"Poor *habibe* has a cold," said Nabila, Ben's not-girlfriend from Egypt. Her nerdy brown eyes looked sadly at Ben through her thick glasses.

Nabila put her tray and Ben's tray in front of Gordon.

"Would you mind smelling ours?" she asked. "As you know, I have—"

"Yeah, yeah," said Gordon as he snatched the trays. "You have no sense of smell. I remember. How convenient."

After two more mega-whiffs, Gordon gave a thumbs-up.

"Okay, visual check," Shane continued.

We all grabbed our forks and began moving our food around to make sure nothing was hiding in the folds. I slowly lifted off the top of my Blandburger and peered inside.

As I replaced the bun, I saw some kid headed our way. He had a full tray of food and it looked like he was planning on sitting at our table. I hated to be cruel, but we couldn't have outsiders listening in on our conversations. It was for their own good.

"Ben," I said while elbowing him. "Someone's coming."

"Not again," said Ben, and he started to make himself gag.

The kid looked at him strangely, but still tried to put his tray down.

Ben's whole body began to spasm as he returned the boy's look. Then it happened.

BLAARRP!

Ben spewed a small splatter of barf onto the table.

The kid slowly backed away and then ran off.

"Okay, *now* are we free to discuss saving the old monsters from monster juice drainage?" yelled Ben as he wiped a few leftover chunks from his mouth.

"You don't have to yell it," said Nabila as she cleaned up his mess. "There are still kids at other tables."

"Sorry," Ben said. "My ears are all clogged."

"Good barfin', buddy," said Gordon, patting Ben on the back. "Perfect targeting. Always the right amount."

"Half the time, I really do need to barf, you know," Ben said, snotting.

"Speaking of barf," Shane added as he poked at his food, "the thought of what's in here makes me want to hurl."

"Are you sure we have to search our food every day?" asked Gordon as he shook at his Pepperphony Pizz-ugh. "So what if Lunch Lady feeds us something again? We'll probably need it to battle a new breed of monster."

"I guess Gordon is right," said Shane. "Chris ate roaches, we beat roaches. We ate zombie piranha, and were better against the underwater skin monsters. But I just wish Lunch Lady would warn us, you know?"

"I still can't believe she fed you sussuroblats," Nabila said to me. "Was it the whole roach? That must have been a big burger. Did she include any lips? I think that's probably where all the magic is . . ."

I gagged at the thought of eating sussuroblat lips. A

bit of barf rose into my mouth and I quickly swallowed it. Another kid who was trying to sit down eyed me with disgust and then changed her mind and headed for another table.

"Aw, thanks," said Ben.

"How was the meeting between your mother and Director Z?" Nabila asked me.

"The good news is that Director Z convinced her nothing strange was going on at the old retirement home before it burned to the ground," I replied. "The bad news is that he did *such* a good job, she asked to hold her next PTA meeting at the new place! She's meeting with him today for a tour, and then Sunday they'll have the meeting."

"I think she's still investigating," said Shane. "Their friendly meeting over tea wasn't enough."

"I agree," I said. "Which is why we all have to make sure nothing goes wrong during the tour. I'm terrified she'll see something that will make her freak. So we *all* need to be there to make sure everything looks perfectly normal—*great*, even."

"Aw, come on!" said Gordon. "I have wrestling practice after school. Didn't Director Z say all the old monsters would be on their best behavior?"

"We've all seen those guys on their 'best behavior,'" said Shane, "and it's the worst."

"It's pretty bad," said Nabila.

"Yep," snorted Ben.

"Arrrgh, I guess you're right," Gordon said, rushing out of his seat. "I'm gonna see if anyone's practicing at the gym right now. See ya later, losers."

Ben blew a huge snot rocket into a tissue, crumpled it up, and tossed it onto Gordon's tray.

"I'm not sure he's finished," said Nabila.

"Well, he's finished now," I said with a chuckle.

"Wow," my mother said as she parked the car. "It's . . . well, it's HUGE! So much bigger than Raven Hill. It's beautiful."

She stared in awe at Gallow Manor Retirement Home as Ben, Shane, Gordon, and I stumbled out of the cramped backseat. The huge stone manor looked like a small castle.

"Just wait until you see what it looks like inside," Nabila said as she got out of the passenger seat. "It's amazing!"

"Be cool, or she'll suspect something is up," I whispered to Nabila. "It's not *that* great."

We walked to the huge, wooden, iron-studded front

door and rang the bell. Beautifully sculpted bushes sat on either side of the door with huge, colorful stained-glass windows above them. I glanced at one of the snow-covered bushes and could have sworn I saw two eyes looking at me through the cold. I did a double take, and by the time I looked back, the eyes were gone.

My mom's visit has me so nervous that I must be seeing things, I thought. *Everyone was warned to be on their best behavior.*

Before I could ask anyone else if they had seen the mysterious eyes, Director Z himself opened the door.

"Mrs. Taylor," said Director Z, pale and skinny, but always well dressed. "It's delightful to see you. Please, come inside from the cold."

My mother eyed every square inch of the foyer as we entered. The marble floors were scuffed, the tapestries on the wall were worn, the fireplace was slightly charred, but at least it didn't look like it could fall down at any time like Raven Hill had. *The best thing that ever happened to that dump was the fire that turned it to ashes*, I thought.

"I specifically said that your services weren't needed tonight," said Director Z, eyeing me.

"Oh, we had a lot of . . . um . . . stuff left over from yesterday," I said.

A few of the residents rolled past in wheelchairs.

Shane waved at Clarice, the banshee, who gave us

a dirty look from behind her walker. The old monsters had gotten stronger since they'd returned from Paradise Island. So we had begged them to act as old as possible for my mother.

"Thanks so much for putting my mind at ease when we spoke before," my mother said as Director Z took her coat. "I just keep thinking of how sad it was that you lost everything because of one faulty light switch."

"We're all dealing with the tragedy as best we can," said Director Z. "I'm lucky to have an amazing nursing staff, and your son and his friends were a huge help during our transition into the new facilities. We're so grateful to have them."

"I'm just so glad that Chris was at Kennedy Space Center when it all happened," said my mother.

She gave me a look that said, *I'm still not sure you were actually there . . .*

A Nurse walked over to grab our coats. Nabila and I gasped when we saw him. Ben sneezed in surprise, and a booger landed with a plop at Gordon's feet.

"What is it?" asked my mother.

He put on a uniform that actually fits, for my mother, I thought. I was used to seeing the Nurses—the massive, doofy men with huge heads who helped keep the old monsters in line—in one-size-too-small nurses' uniforms.

"Oh, nothing," I said as calmly as I could.

"What a beautiful coat, Madam," said the Nurse. "It really brings out the color of your eyes."

This time Shane gasped while my mother blushed at the compliment.

Director Z leaned in and whispered to us, "It took me an entire week to teach him that. So proud! As you can see, I've got everything under control. Your presence really isn't necessary."

The Nurse took the coats and headed to a nearby closet. My mother turned to us just as Director Z leaned back into place.

"What courteous staff you have, Director," said my mother.

"Please," said Director Z, "call me Zachary."

As Director Z and my mother turned and walked ahead of us, I looked behind to see a skeletal hand reach out of the closet and grab our coats from the Nurse.

Here we go, I thought.

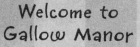

Welcome to Gallow Manor

Director Z led my mother out of the beautiful marbled foyer toward the West Wing. Not knowing what to do, we followed them. After only a few steps, we could hear a pounding behind us.

"It's Roy, the Old Bigfoot," whispered Shane.

"Get outta sight!" Gordon hissed at the monster.

We waved him away frantically, but the shaggy gray bigfoot kept pounding his way toward us. The sour scent of his stinky old feet (which were, in fact, HUGE) increased with each step.

"Director Z?" Old Bigfoot asked. "I've been looking for you all day."

Director Z and my mother stopped.

Before they could turn around, Ben ran up to them and barfed on Director Z's shoes.

"Whhhhhharrrf," said Ben. "I'm so sorry."

"Oh dear," said my mother, too busy with barfy Ben to notice the stinky sasquatch. "Are you okay?"

She leaned down to help Ben.

"Director Z?" Old Bigfoot asked again.

Now Director Z was trying to wave him off, but he kept coming.

Shane ripped down one of the old tapestries, jumped up, and covered Old Bigfoot from head to hairy toes just as my mother turned around.

"My, aren't you just so cold," I said, wrapping the tapestry tightly around him. "Let's get you to your room."

Shane hurriedly shuffled Old Bigfoot off down the West Wing before my mother could see him—or smell him.

The rest of us stood there, staring at my mother and Director Z.

"Soooooo . . . ?" I asked Director Z.

"Yes, it does look like you might have a lot of 'stuff' to deal with." Director Z sighed, shaking Ben's barf off of his shoes. "Why don't you run off and make sure nobody else needs to be taken care of."

I gave Director Z a dirty look and headed down the hallway with my friends.

As soon as Shane had safely plopped Old Bigfoot

back in his room and closed the door, we heard growling from the room in front of us.

"Uh-oh . . . ," said Shane, rushing ahead. "Sounds like someone else is on their 'best behavior.'"

Three mangy old werewolves dragged their butts around a carpeted drawing room with a beautiful fireplace and very expensive antique furniture.

Lamps shook on rickety old tables. Fur was flying everywhere, and the smell was outrageous. The werewolves didn't even look like old dogs anymore—their coats were still somewhat gray, but they had all of their fur back. Not one of them had peed on a rug in weeks.

"Waaaaah-choo!" sneezed Ben, splattering a fine leather chair with snot.

"Guys!" I yelled. "That's disgusting! Stop it! Right now!"

"Arooo—" one started to howl with relief at having his itch scratched, but Shane was able to grab him and clamp his half-toothed mouth shut.

Another one hit one of the tables, and sent a beautiful stained-glass lamp over the edge.

"Eeek," I squealed, rushing forward and catching it just in time.

"Hey!" Ben yelled from the entrance. "They're coming down the hall!"

"Close the door," said Shane.

"There *is* no door," cried Ben.

"Shoot!" I yelled. "Think fast."

"Can you change back into human form?" Shane asked the flea-ridden werewolves.

"Nooooo, wait!" I said, still holding on to the lamp. "They might just keep doing it when they are in human form. Do you want to see that?"

"Ew!" said Gordon.

"Hurry!" said Ben.

Nabila ran over to a creaky old window, unlatched it, and threw it open. There was a terrible screech—paint flakes sprayed everywhere—and the room was filled with a fresh, cold breeze.

"Out!" She pointed to the open window.

The werewolves cocked their heads and stared at her with funny expressions.

We could hear the click of Director Z's perfectly polished dress shoes coming up to the entrance.

"This is gonna be bad," said Ben, scurrying deeper into the room to hide behind a bookcase.

"FETCH!" yelled Gordon, throwing a small stick of wood from the fireplace out of the window.

The werewolves jumped up from the slightly brown carpet, sprinted to the window in a flash, and jumped out one by one. As the last tail cleared the window, my mother and Director Z entered the room.

"We have several sitting rooms with period furniture

and art from the time when this home was constructed. Apparently, it was built by a shipbuilding family from Britain," said Director Z. "Oh, Chris! Do be careful while cleaning that lamp. You would pay dearly if ever you were to break it."

"Of course," I said, finally placing the lamp back on the table. "Just getting the dust off so nobody's sneezing around here."

Ben sneezed from behind the bookcase.

"Oh, Chrissy," said my mother, "you do such wonderful work for these old folks."

"Would you mind closing the window, Nabila?" asked Director Z.

"Of course, Director," said Nabila.

Director Z took a big whiff and stared at the carpet.

I gave him a look that said, *Get her out of here before she notices!*

"Now," said Director Z, quickly leading my mother out of the room. "Shall I show you the music room? Chris tells me you can play piano. Have you ever played a harpsichord?"

They walked across the hallway and opened the door to the music room. As soon as it had shut, we rushed into the hallway.

"We've got to stay ahead of them," I said, panicked, "or my mother might see something!"

We rushed past a number of closed doors. Luckily,

most of the residents had listened to us, and were keeping quiet in their rooms.

We peeked into a sitting room to see a few old folks playing cards, staring at chessboards, quietly talking, or warming themselves in front of the marble fireplace.

"Lookin' good! Lookin' normal!" yelled Shane, giving all the old monsters a big thumbs-up. "All that's left is the dining room, the kitchen, and—"

"The bathroom!" screeched Nabila, pointing farther down the hallway. "Look!"

Up ahead, a steamy green fog poured out of the bathroom. There was no mistaking that smell.

"Swamp gas!" yelled Gordon.

Through the open door, Gil, the swamp creature, happily sang and farted in the shower.

Behind us, my mother and Director Z emerged from the music room. I could feel the hair stand up on the back of my neck. We lined up from wall to wall to keep her from seeing the green cloud down the hallway.

"Let's just take a quick look at this room," said Director Z, leading my mother into the second sitting room. "The fireplace is exquisite."

"We've got to close the bathroom door," I said, and we turned around to see a zombie stumble out of the bathroom.

"Arrgh! Can't *breathe!*" he moaned and passed out on the hallway floor.

"Wow, farts strong enough to knock out a zombie," said Shane. "I'm constantly impressed by Gil."

"No time to be impressed," I yelled. "We've got to move this zombie before my mother walks down the hallway."

"What about the gas?" yelled Nabila.

Gordon rushed up to the zombie, who was still moaning, and quickly dragged him back into the bathroom.

"No!" the zombie wailed. "Barely survived."

"Barely survived?" Gordon said. "Did you forget you're already dead? Just stay low, under the cloud."

Gordon slammed the door shut, cutting off the green cloud, just as my mother and Director Z came out of the second sitting room.

"Now on to the kitchen," said Director Z as they breezed past us.

My mother wrinkled her nose slightly, but didn't say anything.

After a pause, we rushed after them, through the dining room and into the kitchen.

"This is perhaps the most stunning marblework in the entire manor," said Director Z. "Italian marble, very sterile, perfect for preparing meals for those with special needs—and for your PTA members on Sunday."

"Looks clear in here," whispered Shane, patting me on the back.

Before I could finish saying, "WHEW," there was a great SQUUUUEEEAAAK.

The huge wooden door to the walk-in refrigerator slowly swung open in front of my mother. A gnarled hand gripped the dark wood ominously.

My friends and I stood in shock. There was nothing we could do.

Grigore, the vampire, stumbled out clutching a large plastic bag of blood. He was slurping happily on a plastic tube.

"Ahhh!" my mother screamed, jumping back, surprised.

"WHA!" Grigore screeched, just as surprised, and tossed the blood bag up into the air.

"Oh no," said Ben.

"Oh my!" said my mother as the bag fell back down onto the ground with a SPLAT, and sprayed blood all over Grigore's shoes and pants.

"Nooooo!" he yelled. "My blood!!!"

"Blood?" My mother suddenly looked horrified.

Director Z was, for once, stunned.

"Oh . . . ," Grigore said, looking at my mother. "You can't know. You shouldn't know."

He held his right hand in front of him, made his hand into a claw, and squinted into her eyes.

"You are getting very sleepy," he said.

"No," she said. "I'm not."

"Do. Not. See. Meeee . . . ," purred Grigore.

"But you're right in front of me," my mother said, annoyed. "Covered in—"

"Tomato soup!" I interrupted. "Grigore, how many times have I told you—you can only eat at scheduled mealtimes. What a silly old dude, right?"

My friends and I laughed nervously.

I looked at my mother, hoping she'd believe me.

"But he screeched the word *blood* after he dropped what is clearly an IV bag of blood." My mother furrowed her brow in my direction.

"I am deeply sorry that my resident has scared you," said Director Z, "but Grigore really is one of the more—how do I put this without sounding rude—demented patients here. I assure you, this is not normally what happens at my facility."

"I'm not demented," said Grigore, offended. "I—"

Gordon hissed, raised his fist, and gave Grigore a dirty look. My mother was staring too hard at the blood to notice.

"Right . . . right!" screeched Grigore. "I'm the King of Transylvania! That's vhy I thought this delicious tomato soup vas bllllooooooood!"

"Yes," Director Z quickly added with a smile, "and it's a funny coincidence that the bags we serve all our soup in would look like IV bags to you—we find that serving soups directly from a plastic pouch, using a plastic tube to suck, gives our residents a sense of comfort. Spoons are simply too harsh."

We all stared at my mother, wondering if she would believe our terrible story. She stood there with her mouth open, shocked.

She finally turned to me with a look of anger and said, "Chris, what is going on here?"

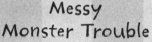

Messy
Monster Trouble

"How could you kids act like this?" my mother scolded. "Are you just going to stand there? Clean the poor old man up!"

"Of course," I said, relieved. "Director Z, where's the cleaning supply closet again?"

"In the back of the dining room," replied Director Z. "Mrs. Taylor, while the children assist Grigore, please allow me to show you the view from the West Tower above the dining room. It's spectacular."

"Yeah, and at night, the stars are amazing out here," I said nervously, trying to get my mother to think about anything but the blood-splattered old vampire in front of her. "I've got my telescope set up in the tower."

"We'll be right back," Shane said to Grigore.

"One of you should stay and keep an eye on him," my mother said.

"Of course," said Nabila. "Ben and I will stay behind."

The rest of us walked out into the dining room.

"Is it this door?" I asked Director Z, who continued walking toward the hallway with my mother.

I grasped the doorknob of the already slightly open door and peeked inside to see bizarre-looking instruments and a huge, grainy photograph of the moon on the wall. The moon had—

"Not that door," said Director Z, who pulled me out of the room before I could explore further. My mother stood in the hallway, looking around at the decorations.

"But the moon," I whispered so my mother didn't hear. "It had a face! Like a real face, not just the craters and hills that make up what we *think* is the face."

"Do you see the moon everywhere, *Moon Boy*?" Gordon said, chuckling.

"It would be best if you forgot about this room for now," Director Z hissed as he closed the door.

Shane opened the next door, revealing a gaggle of mops and every kind of cleaning solution you could imagine.

"This is Ben's dream," said Shane.

"I'm sure it shouldn't take you too long," said Director Z. "Please meet us at the bottom of the stairs and we'll all continue to the East Wing."

He led my mother up the spiral staircase with a warm chuckle.

We grabbed as many supplies as we could and went back into the kitchen to find everything perfectly clean. Nabila and Ben stared wide-eyed at Grigore.

"What happened?" I asked.

Nabila and Ben kept on staring.

"I realized after you left that I could just slurp up all of the blood myself," said Grigore. He stared off into the distance and added, "Like a cat licks up blood."

"Huh?" I said. "You mean like a cat licks up milk?"

"Yes," he said. "Of course that's vhat I meant . . . maybe I am a little demented like the Director says."

Nabila and Ben were finally coming back to the real world.

"You guys okay?" asked Gordon.

"He was so fast," said Nabila. "So creepy."

"And hungry," added Ben, shivering. "I don't think I'm going to be able to sleep tonight."

We left Grigore, and I walked over to the door of the mysterious moon room. It was locked.

"Dang," I said.

"What did you see?" asked Shane.

Before I could answer Shane, Director Z and my mother appeared at the bottom of the stairs.

"Let's head to the other side of the manor, where

there's one room in particular that I think you'd like to see, Mrs. Taylor," said Director Z.

The East Wing was filled with empty rooms. Gallow Manor had a lot of space.

As Director Z led us down the long hallway, organ music blared. It was a louder and darker song than Horace usually played.

We passed by beautiful, dark oil paintings in dusty frames. We passed a suit of armor that stood guard with an ax.

"We have quite a collection of Victorian art. As you can see—"

"WHAT?!" my mother screeched. "I CAN'T HEAR YOU OVER THE MUSIC."

The organ music got crazier and spookier.

"MY APOLOGIES!" Director Z yelled over the music. "I HAD TOLD HORACE NOT TO PRACTICE WHILE YOU WERE HERE, BUT AS YOU KNOW, MANY OF OUR RESIDENTS ARE HARD OF HEARING."

"THAT WOULD EXPLAIN THE VOLUME," my mother yelled back.

But Director Z and I both knew that Horace had amazing hearing. Something else was going on here.

"RUN UP AHEAD AND TELL HIM TO SHUT UP," I yelled to Gordon with a panicked look that said, *Be careful.*

The closer we got to the banquet hall, the louder it got. My mother and I covered our ears. Director Z pretended not to notice. My teeth rattled in my mouth.

Gordon opened the door . . .

. . . and the last note from the organ echoed through a massive banquet hall.

"Well," said my mother, gasping at the beautiful banquet hall as the rest of us came through the door. "This is quite nice."

"Horace?" My squeak echoed off the high arched ceiling.

Huge iron chandeliers hung above a beautiful wood floor, and all around the room was a balcony. In the back, above a stage, was a massive set of pipes, with a small keyboard below.

But the organ player was nowhere to be seen. And the only way out was through the door behind us.

My look of concern made Director Z speak before I could.

"So, Mrs. Taylor," he said, perfectly calm. "We can arrange seating for a number of different occasions. I assume our collection of one hundred folding chairs will work for your PTA meeting?"

"Wow," she gasped, clearly forgetting the fact that an organist had just pulled a disappearing act. "Yes."

"Wonderful," Director Z said, clapping his hands together. "Then we'll make all the preparations necessary for your big day on Sunday. Chris, you and your friends should come extra early tomorrow."

As we were leaving Gallow Manor, I noticed Horace walking down the hallway to the West Wing. I rushed over to speak with him.

"Was there a secret door?" I asked. "Is that how you got out so quick?"

"Pardon?" he asked, looking confused.

"In the banquet hall just now you were playing a crazy, loud song that ended right when we opened the door."

"I don't know what you're talking about," said Horace. "I just woke up from a nap. The Director gave me strict instructions to lay off the playing while your mother was here."

"Really?" I asked. "That's so strange . . ."

"Chrissy," shrieked my mother from outside, "let's get going!"

The mystery would have to wait.

The Calm
Before the Storm

Early the next morning, Ben, Nabila, Shane, Gordon, and I arrived back at Gallow Manor to help set up the banquet hall for the PTA meeting.

"I'm so excited to spend the day with the monsters," said Nabila as she pulled a handkerchief from her fluorescent pink fanny pack. She handed it to Ben, who couldn't stop sneezing. "I really like the idea of working *with* them, rather than *for* them."

"It depends on the monster," said Gordon. "Murray is always so cranky, Griselda is bossy, and Grigore is plain batty. Not to mention the zombies are . . . well . . . *zombies*."

"I'm just happy that the monsters are finally doing something other than drooling," Shane said. "You saw how helpful they were during the move. All the monsters are getting stronger."

"Yeah, but they're still old," said Ben. "They just went from insanely ancient to just plain old."

"But if we do have another attack," Shane said, "they should be strong enough to fight. I've been teaching them some moves."

"I don't even want to think about another attack," I said. "I just want to survive this PTA meeting without my mother attacking."

"I don't know about surviving your mother," said Director Z, who had walked up to the entrance of the banquet hall to meet us, "but it would be hard for someone to attack the manor. We have extra protection in the main facility with a deep dungeon to fall back into if we need it. But we won't need it with the charms and seals that have been put on the facility. And Shane and Gordon's emergency action plans have all been memorized by the residents, who, I assure you, are ready for a fight if it happens."

Someone on the other side of the hall huffed. We turned to see Murray standing at a podium. He waved his wrapped hand dismissively at Director Z.

"It doesn't matter what you do, Zachary," said Murray. "We're all done for. The great lebensplasm drinker in the sky will take every last one of us before all is said and done."

"What's got into Hotep?" Shane said while pointing his thumb toward the podium.

"I don't know how many times I have to tell you," grumbled Murray. "My name is Murray. Not Hotep."

"You've got to be kidding. Murray's not a mummy name," said Shane. "It just doesn't feel right. You're totally Hotep."

Gordon snickered. "Told you Murrayhotep was a grump! He barely helped the other monsters move into this place—half the time he had disappeared to who-knows-where."

"Well, I'll have you know—" Murray started to say.

"Let it be, Murray," Director Z said. "We have a lot to accomplish before the parents and teachers arrive."

"You always side with the humans, Zachary," Murray said as he stormed out of the hall. "This is why you will always fail."

My first job was to clear out the massive sections of giant spiderwebs that covered most of the hall. I stood with a broom and a pair of hedge clippers as I stared down at least a half dozen fist-size spiders.

"I told you guys that the East Wing is off limits today!" I said to the agitated spiders.

In unison they shook their hairy spider legs at me and then reared up, exposing insanely long and pointy fangs.

"I have to take down your webs," I continued. "There's no way around this."

Griselda, the head witch, approached with a small black bag.

"All right," she cackled, "I need a refill of leg-of-spider. Any volunteers?"

The spiders quickly formed a line and scurried out of the door.

"Ve need three more chairs over here," called Grigore, who was helping set up the seating.

Shane rushed over to him with three more chairs.

"It's great to see us all working as a team," sniffled Ben as he helped set up the catering table. Nabila smiled at him as she came over to help with the chairs.

A few zombies ambled aimlessly past her, shuffling chairs from place to place. Nabila huffed and said, "That's good, Jane and John. Just open up the rest of the chairs—I'll straighten things up."

I dodged the zombies and made my way over to Director Z, who was adjusting the podium. Across the hall Gordon waved his arms, trying to get my attention. He was fiddling with the speakers.

I grabbed the microphone. "Testing, testing, one, two, three . . ."

Gordon gave me a thumbs-up from the back row.

"Awesome," he said as he jogged over. "Now that we're finished setting up, I can play fetch with the werewolves in the North Wing. That hallway is HUGE!"

"Not so quick," said Director Z. "We have a few errands to run."

"What!?" the five of us said at the same time.

"Speaking of werewolves," continued Director Z, "we need to go to the pet store in town to pick up chew toys, and Medusa's snakes are almost down to their last mouse. We should probably head to the butcher's and the blood bank as well. That's a lot to carry, and I'll need all of you to help."

"How are we getting there?" asked Nabila.

"We'll take the company car," Director Z replied.

We all looked at the Director in shock.

"You have a car?" asked Nabila. "Why didn't you tell us? This whole time, you could have picked us up and saved our parents the trouble."

"Did you think I just walked around to get from place to place?" Director Z asked. "Of course we have a car. I just don't like to take it out that often, and I don't think your parents would appreciate it if I started picking you up in it."

"Why?" asked Nabila.

"You'll see," he replied, and motioned us out the door.

We walked to a beautiful carriage house off the east side of the manor. It had three huge wooden doors. The one in the center was open, and inside was a brand-new, sparkly and clean . . .

"Hearse?" Shane chuckled. "Okay, I can see why you don't take this out too often."

Ben gulped. "I don't think I can ride in this."

Director Z opened the back door to reveal an old coffin.

"Like I said," Ben mumbled as he choked something back down, "I don't think I can ride in this."

"You can ride in the front with me," said Director Z.

"Is anybody . . . ," Nabila said and pointed at the coffin.

"No," Director Z replied, but then a funny look came over his face. "Well, maybe. You might want to knock."

We all piled into the hearse, and Director Z reversed it out of the carriage house. Before he was able to turn down the road, a Nurse jumped in front of the car.

Director Z slammed on the brakes. All of us, and the coffin, slid up toward the front seats.

"Boss," the Nurse said, knocking on the window, "we've lost Murray and Grigore. Again. They should be helping us with the food, but we can't find them anywhere!"

"I'm sure they'll wander back," said Director Z. "Until the residents get used to this place, they're going to keep getting lost. Have three Nurses check each wing."

A creaking sound came from the back of the hearse. A gnarled hand made its way out from below the cover of the coffin.

"Wha!? Guys!!" Nabila squealed, backing away from the coffin.

Whatever Ben had choked down earlier erupted down the front of his shirt.

"I'm here," croaked Grigore. "I'm just a little down. It's just I . . . I vas thinking about somevone I'd lost . . . and vas trying to hide avay."

"See," said Director Z as he slowly pulled the car away from the Nurse, "we've found one already. Go back to bed, Grigore. Everything is fine."

Two hours later the hearse pulled back into the carriage house. Gordon was slumped in his seat. He had been terrified that someone from the team would see him riding around in the big, black death boat. Once Director Z turned off the ignition, Gordon practically jumped out of the car, yelling, "Pietro! Howie! Calling all mangy mutts for a game in the North Wing hallway."

"Gordon," I yelled. "Aren't you going to help carry anything?"

"No time," he called back.

"Just be careful in the manor," Director Z added. "If you break anything, you'll pay for it."

That's strange, I thought, *we've broken plenty of things in the past and he never made us pay for anything. Now he's mentioned it twice.*

Shane struggled to get out of the hearse, holding on to a huge bag that squirmed and squeaked.

"Hey," he said, and I gave him a little push through the door. "Do you remember when we had to hand-feed the mice to poor Medusa's snakes? Now they're chomping at us before we can even get the package open."

"Things have certainly changed," I said. "I think—"

Spray from a wet sneeze blew across my face. Nabila whipped out her handkerchief and offered it to me.

"Sorry," Ben snorted. "We should probably go soon. I've run out of allergy medication."

"I'll call my mother after we catch up with Gordon. I might want to toss a few balls myself," I said.

The werewolves were going crazy in the North Wing.

"FETCH!" yelled Gordon. He tossed a large red rubber ball, and the three werewolves went tearing down the huge hallway, which was as wide as a small soccer field.

They nipped at each other, and then one of them ran back to Gordon with the ball.

"Can I try?" I asked.

"Sure," said Gordon.

"I'm next," said Shane.

"Make sure to throw it really far, or they'll just stand there and wait for you to try again," said Gordon.

"Oooof," I yelped as I tossed the ball as far as I could.

The three werewolves went scurrying off with a howl.

One grabbed the ball and came running back at me . . . FAST!

"Wait," I said. "Slow down!"

Faster and faster he ran, until he knocked my feet out from under me. I fell into Ben, sending him headfirst into a pedestal that held a large vase.

"Are you okay?" asked Shane as he picked me up.

Ben was holding on to the pedestal for dear life. But the vase jiggled as Ben swayed, trying to steady himself—it had edged right to the side.

"Don't move!" said Shane as he headed for Ben.

Ben's eyes widened, and I noticed his nose begin to twitch. "Ahh . . . ," he said. "AAAAAAH . . ."

"Whatever you do," I said, moving in behind Shane, "don't finish that sneeze."

"CHOOOOOOO!"

He shook the pedestal violently, knocking the vase over in a shower of snot. Shane dove to catch it, but the snot-covered vase slipped through his fingers and smashed into a million pieces.

"Sorry," coughed Ben. "I told you we should have gone home."

Shane sat up and wiped his boogery fingers on Ben's shirt. "Do you have any superglue in that fanny pack of yours?" he asked Nabila.

"Something tells me this is beyond superglue," I said.

Before we could figure out what to do, the whole hallway began to shake. The candelabras on the wall vibrated and jerked in and out. The windows rattled. Instinctively, the werewolves tucked their tails and ran.

Then a scream came from somewhere within the walls and echoed through the hallway.

"AAAAAARRRGGGGGHHHHH!"

A gate slammed down behind us, sealing us in from the rest of the manor.

We were trapped!

The Storm Before the Calm

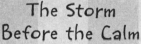

"Weeeee. Wiiiiilllll. DESTROY. Youuuuuuu."

After sitting trapped in the hallway for what seemed like an eternity, we were starting to make out what the voices in the hallway were saying.

"We?" asked Shane. "Who are you?"

"It's not the 'we' part that's bothering me," Ben added. "It's the whole 'destroy you' bit that is freaking me out."

"We won't be able to stop them if we don't know who they are," Shane replied.

"Yeah, why won't you show yourselves?" I screamed.

"I wouldn't question them," Nabila said. "It might anger them further."

41

Just then a wind picked up, and the tiny pieces of the broken vase swirled like a small tornado.

"Cover your eyes," I called out.

"The dust!" Ben squealed. "I can barely breathe!"

Nabila ran to Ben while Gordon ran to the gate that blocked the hallway and shook the iron railings like a crazed prisoner, trying to escape.

The tornado headed for us, and we all backed up against the gate.

"There has to be a switch!" I yelled over the howling wind. "A lever! Something!"

Shane, Gordon, and I frantically searched for a way out while Nabila dealt with Ben, who was having a full-on allergy attack. She handed him an inhaler from her fanny pack as he collapsed at the bottom of the gate.

"Guys, we have to get him out of here!" yelled Nabila. Her hair whipped in the wind.

"Over here," yelled Gordon. "I think I've found it!"

The tornado had almost reached us. Shane and I had to struggle against the wind to get to Gordon, who was struggling with a small iron door. Shards of the vase whizzed past us, one or two cutting small slits into my pant leg.

"That tornado is going to tear us to shreds if we don't hurry," I said.

As the three of us struggled to open the door, the wind howled, "NOOOOOOOOOOO!"

The small iron door sprung open so fast we were thrown onto the floor. Shane jumped back up and pulled down the lever that was inside.

With a great creak and a rattle, the iron gate began to rise.

As it rose, the tornado shot back down the hallway and blew a window open. The pieces of vase blew out and into the sky and met with dark clouds.

Lightning struck the window, which closed with a BAM.

The wind stopped and the gate was now fully open.

"Let's get out of here," I said. "This place is haunted!"

As we scurried into the main marble foyer, Director Z came up to us with a concerned look on his face.

"I saw the werewolves run past," Director Z said, "and I heard a terrible racket—is everyone okay? Did you break anything?"

"Oh, man," said Gordon. "We were playing fetch, and—"

"Just got a little too aggressive," Nabila interrupted. "Ben got overwhelmed with the dust and running."

Gordon and Ben looked at her funny, but we let her keep going.

"You probably heard the thunder," she continued. "Wasn't that strange?"

As if to back up her story, another bolt of lightning struck the grounds and shook the manor.

"I see," said Director Z. "Ben, are you okay?"

Ben slumped against Gordon. He tried to speak, but could only cough out a glop of orange boogers—the same color as the vase. He smiled weakly and gave Director Z a thumbs-up.

"I think we need to get him out of here," Nabila said.

"Yeah, let's get him a little fresh air," I said, and headed for the door.

I turned the old brass handle, and an icy chill shot up my arm. The door blew open, knocking me back. As I hit the floor the first thing I noticed wasn't the pain of my rear, but of snow hitting me in the face. A lot of snow.

"Whoa," I said as I slid into Shane, my butt rippling over the marble.

A few Nurses came in and forced the door closed, but even they had trouble finally getting it to shut all the way.

For a moment it was insanely quiet—then my phone rang.

Everyone stared at me as I answered it.

"Hello?" I said.

It was my mother.

"Are you ready, Chrissy?" she asked. "I'll come and get you now."

"Mom," I screeched, still winded from everything

44

that had happened. "You can't drive in this!"

"Drive in what, honey?" she asked.

"The blizzard. The thundersnow!" I said.

"Chrissy, the sky is blue," she said, sounding confused.

"Well, it's snowing like crazy here. You'll never get over the bridge," I said.

Director Z motioned for me to hand him the phone.

He grabbed it and said, as calm as could be, "Mrs. Taylor, I must admit, I have never seen snow like this before."

He looked out of the window and continued, "It must have started only ten minutes ago, and there's nearly an inch on the ground already. I can't even see past the driveway. I don't think you should pick up the children. The sun sets soon, and the roads must be terrible."

A few *mmmm-hmmm*s later, Director Z handed me back my phone.

"Chrissy, I don't like this," she said. "But if what Zachary says is true, I really shouldn't come out there."

"Don't worry, Mom," I said, trying to be as calm as Director Z. "You'll see us in the morning, anyway."

My cell phone went dead.

"Mom? MOM!?"

With a soft whirring sound, all the lights dimmed and went out.

"Yipppeee!" an old monster yelled from the West Wing.

As the sun set, the snow picked up. I wanted nothing more than to get out of this haunted house.

No-Sleepover

"Looks like we're having a sleepover," Shane said as we watched the snow pile up outside the window.

"Yeah, it should be fun," I added, smiling at Ben, whose breathing hadn't gotten much better. He smiled back, knowing that I was just trying to cheer him up.

"Why don't you sleep in the music room?" suggested Director Z, handing out candles in tarnished old candelabras. "I believe that it's been soundproofed, so the storm might not bother you as much. I'll have the chefs prepare hot chocolate."

"That sounds good for the boys," Nabila said, "but I think it would be best if I slept in my own room."

"Of course," said Director Z. "You can take the room

across from the music room when it's time to sleep."

"But, Nabila," snorted Ben. "Will you be okay?"

"I'll be just fine on my own, thank you very much, *habibe*," she said.

"Do you *remember* what happened in that hallway?" Ben whispered with concern to Nabila. "This place is crazy haunted!"

"So far, we only know that there was something mysterious happening with the vase," she whispered back confidently. "I'll be right across the hall."

"Ben," said Director Z, "I'll get one of the witches to brew an antihistamine potion. You certainly look like you could use it."

As Director Z left, we all turned to Nabila. Before any of us could ask her, she replied to the question that she knew was coming.

"I lied about the vase because Director Z said that we would have to pay if we broke anything. Did you see how old that vase was? It must be extremely expensive. Plus, he'll probably never notice. Whatever tried to kill us did us the favor of blowing the mess out into the sky."

"Yeah, but I'm worried whatever *that* was didn't leave with the vase," I said.

"Well, I, for one, am glad that Nabila didn't tell the truth," said Shane. "I don't get enough allowance to buy new nineteenth-century artifacts."

Hours later, after Nabila had gone to her room, Shane, Ben, Gordon, and I sat in the music room. The candelabras rested on the floor, making our shadows jump around the room.

Ben was completely asleep, knocked out from Griselda's antihistamine potion. He clutched his now-empty hot chocolate mug.

"Hey, isn't that the same potion that amped me up?" asked Gordon.

"Yeah," said Shane. "But you had just taken a six-hour nap in a sea worm."

"True . . . true," replied Gordon.

"Okay, guys," I said, blowing out the candles. "Let's get some sleep. We have a big day tomorrow."

We all lay down. The room was insanely dark. And insanely quiet. Too quiet. Nobody said anything for ten minutes, and then . . .

"This place is giving me the creeps," said Gordon. "All I can hear is my heart beating; I think I'm about to go crazy."

"Yeah," I said.

"I dunno," said Shane. "I think quiet is good. Relaxing. Maybe this place isn't haunted after all."

There were a few more moments of silence, and then a harpsichord started to play quietly in the dark.

"Hey, did your mother finally teach you how to play the piano?" Shane asked.

"Noooooo . . . ," I said.

"It's not me," Gordon said.

I tried not to screech as I fumbled for the matches. As I struck the first, I saw we were alone.

"Whew," said Shane, his eyes searching the dimly lit room. "I thought someone was in here."

"You're not worried the harpsichord is playing itself?" Gordon asked.

"Why would I? It's a sweet piece. Probably French. Baroque," Shane said.

Gordon looked under the harpsichord. "It's plugged in or something, right?"

"The power's out," I replied. "Duh!"

I had finally lit the three candles on my candelabra and held it high.

"Gordon, watch out," I yelled.

A guitar floated past Gordon's head—he ducked to avoid it.

It played along with the harpsichord, and both instruments got louder and louder.

"Okay, this isn't so fun anymore," Shane said. "My ears are ringing."

"Let's try to stop it," I said, and lunged toward the harpsichord.

Gordon followed, trying to silence the guitar.

But they got so loud that we were stopped in our tracks, it hurt so much.

"How is Ben sleeping through this?" I asked.

"Let's get Director Z," said Shane. "He'll know how to handle this."

We filed out into the hallway.

"Should someone stay with Ben?" I asked.

SLAM!

The door closed, and all we could hear was the storm, which raged on.

"I guess not," I said.

We rushed down the hall to Director Z's room, but before we could open his door, there was a scream from the foyer.

"That sounds like Nabila," said Gordon.

Forgetting Director Z for the moment, we rushed into the foyer, but didn't see Nabila. We kept moving, jogging into the East Wing, only to find the portrait of Lucinda B. Smythe in a tizzy.

"No matter what I do," she said, "those other portraits keep staring at me!"

She pointed across the hall to the portraits that hung on the wall. They really did stare at you, no matter which way you moved.

"I had a Nurse move me today, but it's no use," she said. "This place is haunted with wicked spirits! They taunt me so!"

"That was you screaming?" I asked Lucinda. "You haven't seen Nabila around, have you?"

"I'm right here," she said, wiping the sleep out of her eyes with one hand and holding her candelabra with the other. "What's going on?"

"Were you sleeping?" Shane asked. "Because our room is a little too haunted for such activities."

"Yeah, can we please sleep in your room?" asked Gordon. "Let's get out of here."

"Where's Ben?" she asked.

"In the music room," I said. "Griselda's potion knocked him out."

"Let's drag him into my room, too," she said.

Before we could head back, a low moan and metallic rattling filled the hall. We looked in the direction of the foyer and saw a suit of armor shake centuries of dust out of its joints and turn toward us.

Someone or SOMETHING was inside the armor.

"Grigore?" asked Shane. "Pietro? Is that you?"

"Waaarrrggghhh," came the garbled reply.

"Really funny," laughed Shane. "Well done."

Gordon, Nabila, and I backed down the hall toward the banquet hall.

With a loud CREAK the armor raised the huge ax that it held.

"Uh, Shane," I said. "I don't think this is a joke."

"Yeah, maybe not," gasped Shane, and we started running.

Behind us, we heard the sound of groaning, clanking metal as the armor pulled its feet off of the pedestal it was nailed to and clanged down the hallway, ax raised high.

"Hurry, Shane!" I yelled. "It's right behind you!"

"GWAAAAAHHHH!" yelled the armor.

Gordon, Nabila, and I ran into the banquet hall and grabbed the two heavy doors, ready to slam them shut.

Shane dashed through and we pushed with all of our might. The doors crashed to a close just as the ax sliced into the wood.

Eventually, there was a clanking of metal as the suit of armor walked away. All we could hear was our heavy breathing and the storm raging outside until . . .

"I told you so," screeched Lucinda from the other side of the door.

We sat huddled in the middle of the banquet hall

around the candelabra, trying to figure out our next move.

"Are we sure there's not another way out of this room?" asked a frustrated Gordon.

"We could climb out of a window," said Nabila.

I peered out of a window and gritted my teeth.

"It looks like the windows are almost covered in snow," I said. "You might freeze before you get to the front door."

"Maybe we can just run past him. His ax is in the door," said Shane.

"Wasn't there an arsenal of weapons hanging next to him?" asked Nabila.

"Right," I said. "But I think we have to try anyway."

Shane walked stealthily to the door, and tried to open it.

"It won't budge. It's either locked or the ax has jammed it, or both," he said.

"Drat," I said, and fell back onto the cold floor.

It was three in the morning, and the snow had completely covered the windows. I huddled in front of a single candle. We were lighting them one at a time in hopes of making them last until daybreak. The others were asleep, and it was my turn to stand guard. I'd begun to nod off when I heard a terrible roar in the hallway. It woke me up fast, and I skittered over to Shane.

"Hey," I said. "Pssst! Wake up. There's something at the door."

BLLLUUUURRG!

Another roar floated into the room from the hallway.

"SHANE! WAKE UP!"

Shane jumped up and swayed on his feet. "Whaytuh?"

"There's something at the door," I said.

Gordon and Nabila were slowly waking up as well.

At the door, the strange creature gave another BLLLUUUURRG and the ax was pulled out of the wood.

"It sounds like a sussuroblat," said Shane.

"Oh, man," said Gordon, his teeth chattering. "I hope not."

The doorknob started to turn.

"Do sussuroblats know how to open a door?" Shane asked.

Gordon jumped over to one of the folding chairs that had been set up for tomorrow's PTA meeting and ran back to the door with it over his head.

"Whhhhhaaaa!" he yelled.

"BLLLLUUURRRGGGHH!" yelled the creature as it opened the door.

Gordon brought the chair down as hard as he could, and—

"Wait!" Nabila yelled. "It's Ben! *Habibe!*"

Gordon threw the chair to the right at the last minute, where it hit the wall with a CRASH.

"Hey, gggggguuysssss," gurgled Ben. "I woke up with a *masssssssiifff sneeeezzzz*, and spent an hour looking for you. Nabila, can I have a handkerchief? I'm dying over here. BLUUUUURGGH!"

Ben walked into the room, and the doors swung shut behind him with a click.

Gordon ran up to the door and grabbed the handles.

"Nooooooo!" he screamed. "It's locked! I gotta peeeeeee!!!"

"Welcome to the party," Shane said to Ben.

PTA Come and Play

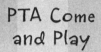

The sun rose on a new day at Gallow Manor. We had survived the night, but in the banquet hall, Gordon was struggling.

"Man, if someone doesn't show up soon, I'm gonna have to pee all over this place," he said.

"You could just blame it on the werewolves," said Shane.

"They stopped doing that," I said.

Gordon rushed to a wall and unzipped his fly.

"Gross," said Nabila.

"I have no choice!" Gordon sounded desperate.

There was a click at the door, and it slowly creaked open. Gordon swiftly zipped back up.

Director Z walked in with a scowl on his face.

"What are you doing fooling around?" asked Director Z. "The PTA meeting is in less than two hours."

"How are they even going to get here?" I asked. "There's four feet of snow out there."

"Take a look outside," said Director Z.

Shane and I ran up to the window. The snow had melted enough to look out the very top. Shane gave me a boost so I could have a peek.

"WHOA," I said.

"What?" asked Shane, looking up.

"Dude," I replied. "The snow ends ten feet past the manor. Even the parking area is completely clear."

"I've never seen snow so localized," said Director Z, "and I have a theory about what has caused this. But we don't have time for that now. I must check in with Lunch Lady and make sure the proper preparations are being made."

I opened my mouth to tell Director Z what had happened to us the night before, but he cut me off.

"I suggest you all take showers," said Director Z. "But you'll need to unclog the drains and clean up the bathroom first. Gil decided to take another three-hour-long swamp shower to keep warm last night. There's swamp muck and vegetation everywhere, and we can't let our guests see such a mess."

Frederick, the old stitched-together monster, came

in holding a bizarre-looking metal cylinder with rubber on the tips.

"Here you go, Boss," he said, and handed the cylinder to Director Z.

"Thank you," said Director Z. "Frederick and I have been laboring over this particular piece of plumbing equipment for quite some time, and it should help you out greatly with unclogging the drains. Simply insert the front end into the drain, make sure to hold on to the rubber at the top, and press the red button. It utilizes a quite powerful type of electricity, so please make sure you're not actually *in* the water when using it."

"Got it," said Shane, snatching the electro de-clogger. "Should we expect any alligators?"

"Not this time," said Director Z, and he turned to leave.

"Aw, man," said Shane as we followed Director Z.

We quickly showered and then put on the same clothes we had worn the day before. Ben did his best to clean off the puke and orange boogers.

"Did you find any shampoo?" Ben asked as Shane

walked into the room drying his hair. "I couldn't use anything because of my allergies."

"The only thing I found was the werewolves' flea and tick shampoo," said Shane. "Which is good, because I think they might have given me fleas a few months back, and I'd been meaning to do something about that."

Gordon squirmed on the bench in front of the harpsichord.

"What's wrong with you?" I asked.

"I can't STAND wearing the same underwear two days in a row," Gordon shouted. "It just feels *wrong*."

"Hey," Ben said, squinting. "Is that something green poking out of your butt crack?"

"What?!" Gordon reached back and pulled a huge wad of swamp vegetation out of his pants. "Awwwww, man!"

Nabila walked into the room, looking fresh and clean.

"That's why I always carry an extra pair of underwear in my fanny pack," she said. "You never know. Next time I'll carry a second extra pair for you, Gordon."

"Umm . . ." Gordon looked confused. "Thanks?"

When we got back to the banquet hall, Lunch Lady and a few chefs—men who looked like Nurses, but with chefs' hats instead of nurses' caps—started to bring out the food that Lunch Lady had prepared.

One chef came into the room with a huge bowl of whitefish to spread on the bagels.

"Hey," said Ben, grabbing the bowl, "this is regular fish, right? It's not zombie piranha salad . . . right?"

"Just don't geet any snot in eet," said Lunch Lady. "You really should just lie down, my darleeng."

She grabbed the bowl and put it in the center of the table. Jane the zombie shuffled into the room and was about to grab a handful of the whitefish for a snack when Nabila pulled a bit of vegetable brain out of her fanny pack and jumped in front of her.

"Hungry?" she asked, as she waved the vegetable brain in front of Jane.

The zombie swiped the brain and gulped it down as she shuffled off.

"Hey," said Shane, "you're getting better at handling the zombies than me these days."

"Thanks," she said.

"I'm sure it helps that Ben has got so much snot in his brain that he's part zombie," Gordon said, chuckling.

We shuffled the last of the zombies out of the room just in time for the first parents and teachers to arrive, escorted by Nurses.

"Thank you so much for coming," Director Z said as

each one arrived. "I hope you don't mind being escorted to this room, but our new facility is quite large, and I'd hate for you to get lost."

The parents and teachers were very impressed with the facilities.

"Wow," said one, "this is massive!"

"Hey," said another. "Ms. Veracruz, what are you doing here?"

"Where are the old folks?" asked another.

"Oh," said Director Z, "we didn't feel the need to bother them with your activities, nor you with theirs. They're most likely in their common area, or their rooms."

I stood next to Shane and Gordon, handing out the agendas that my mother had printed up. Nabila was tending to Ben, who was still super snotty.

My mother arrived, took one look at the setup, and gave me a big thumbs-up!

"Chrissy," she said, "I can't believe the snow. We didn't get one bit. It's like it just all dumped on the retirement home. Until I saw it with my own eyes, I thought you'd made it up."

"Totally weird, right?" I replied. "It was a crazy night."

"The food looks great," she said. "How does the lunch lady know Director Z?"

"It's a long story," I said. "I'll tell it to you sometime."

Once everyone had grabbed a little breakfast and settled in, my mother stood up and headed for the podium.

"Good morning, everyone," she said. "It's so great to have you all here. Please refer to the agenda you were handed, and let's get started."

The meeting began, and everything seemed okay. I even started to relax. The five of us sat in the back of the banquet hall in a circle of chairs we had gathered. We played the game of pretending to squeeze the tiny heads of teachers we didn't like between our fingers. Then we saw Mr. Stewart's bushy head of hair and had a fun time squishing his head even though we liked him so much.

The more the meeting dragged on, the more I thought we'd get out of it with no problem.

"Maybe this section of the manor isn't haunted," I whispered to Shane.

"Maybe not," he said. "Nothing happened once we got in here last night."

There was a squeak, and the door swung open.

Murrayhotep walked into the room and looked around.

"Thanks again for the help yesterday," said Shane.

Murrayhotep gave Shane a dirty look, and a few of the parents in the back row SHUSHed Shane as some other parent made a big point at the podium.

"What is that grump doing here?" asked Gordon.

Before we could ask Murrayhotep what he was doing, my mother began speaking from the podium again.

"I just wanted to take a moment to thank Gallow Manor Retirement Home for hosting us today," she said, smiling. "I'd especially like to thank my son and his friends for all the preparations they made over the last few days. They do an amazing job volunteering here at the retirement home. Come on up, guys, and take a bow."

We looked at each other in disbelief and then shuffled up to the stage behind the podium. The audience of parents and teachers applauded.

Murrayhotep stomped his way up the center aisle toward us, his right hand raised.

"An amazing job, my eye! These kids are no good," yelled Murray, and dipped his hand into the bag that he was carrying. "Always bothering us. They—"

Before I could yell at Murray for being such a grump, the mic started to produce feedback terribly.

SCCCRRREEEEEEEEEEEE!

We all stood back from the microphone, but it didn't help.

EEEEEEEEEEEEEEEE!

Murrayhotep stopped in his tracks.

The audience covered its ears.

My mother tried to move the microphone, but it didn't help.

Nothing helped.

"Where's Zachary?" she yelled, and jumped off the stage—

Just as four terrifying creatures floated down from the ceiling with a bone-chilling roar.

The Fish Sat Out Too Long

Parents and teachers gasped as four huge, bodiless heads descended from the ceiling. Their long, barbed tongues lashed out from behind sharp tusks.

"I guess this corner of the manor is haunted after all." Shane gulped, dodging the dirty, insanely long and thick black hair that grew out of each head.

Murrayhotep ran back down the aisle in the direction he'd come from. The doors slammed behind him as he left.

"This must be the newest breed of super monster," yelled Gordon. "Murrayhotep is scared to death!"

The creatures growled and slowly circled the five of us as we grouped together on the stage. Drool dripped off of their tusks, and their massive eyes bulged.

In the audience, the parents and teachers chattered nervously. I looked around for my mom, but couldn't find her. Nobody quite knew what they were looking at—or what to do.

"Which action plan?" screeched Nabila. "Which action plan!?"

"Five?" Ben sounded doubtful.

All at once, the creatures opened their mouths with the loudest roar yet. One floated out over the audience, taunting the parents and teachers. Folks were now running to the door.

"It's locked!" someone screamed.

The remaining heads closed in on us on the stage.

"Seven?" Shane sounded desperate. "All of our action plans use old monsters, and they're not here!"

"Just get ready," I said.

"For what?" Gordon asked.

"I dunno—just get ready to defend yourself," I said. "Kick some heads, Shane!"

We were completely cornered, but we had to do something.

"Everyone, please calm down," shouted Director Z as he headed for the locked doors.

Another creature head broke away from the stage and taunted the screaming crowd near the doors.

"WWWWEEEEYYYYYAH!" It moaned and spat.

Shane pulled a few karate moves on the creature heads when they dipped into his space, but they always knew right when to swing out of the way.

"If I keep missing, I'm going to pull a muscle," he said. He finally kicked one right in the jaw, and it flew back onto the floor, a jumble of hair and tusks.

"Waaaa!" squealed Nabila. "One's got Ben!"

Arms had sprouted from the hideous face of another creature, and grabbed Ben, who was now two feet off the ground and rising.

"Guys, help!" he yelled as he rose farther up.

"There. Isss. No. Help. For. YOUUUUU," moaned the head.

"Waaaah," screamed Ben.

Nabila grabbed at his feet.

The head shook Ben violently, and as it did, dust poured out of its long mane. Ben, stuck in the middle of the cloud, took in a huge breath.

"AHHHHH . . .

"AHHHHHHHHHH . . .

"AHHHHHHHHHHHHHHH . . .

"Chooooooooooooooooo!" Ben slobbered and snotted onto the creature's face. I could see a booger stuck on the bulging eye of the creature.

"Ah!" yelled the head as it dropped Ben on the floor with an OOF. "The terrible bogies! My eyes! BLECH! Why, I've never in my life, or my afterlife, seen a snottier sneeze. Dear boy, learn how to cover your mouth! ACK!"

The doors sprang open, pushing the parents and teachers back into the center of the room. The creature that had held Ben floated awkwardly past them and out of the room.

The other floating creatures seemed confused, but quickly followed.

None of the parents knew what to do.

It was deathly silent.

Ben sneezed another violent sneeze on the stage, and was knocked back onto his butt.

We all stood frozen—dumbfounded. Our open jaws nearly touched the floor. For Shane, Gordon, Nabila, and me, it was because we couldn't believe what had just happened. For Ben, it was because he was still choking on the dust. Nabila went over to help him.

The parents and teachers were all dumbfounded as well. They all sat back down, and everyone looked at us with their heads cocked to the side.

I was still standing in the middle of it all, so all eyes were on me. Gordon and Shane backed down from the stage.

"Uhhhhhmmmm . . . ," I said.

Durrrrrrrrrrrr . . . , thought my brain.

Before anyone could say anything, Director Z walked forward from the back of the room, clapping loudly.

"Bravo! Bravo!" he called. A few of the parents turned around and watched him come their way. "What an excellent performance. So gut-wrenching, powerful . . . realistic! Ladies and gentlemen, please give the wonderful St. James Players and many of your own children a round of applause for the amazing theater piece they just performed. What amazing acting!"

"This. Isn't. Act. Ing," Ben coughed.

"Ah, but you are too modest," countered Director Z. He squinted his eyes at me and nodded his head that I should talk.

"Yes," I said. "Ladies and gentlemen, thank you so much for watching our new play: *Horror at Gallow Manor.* We hope we've entertained you this afternoon!"

The room was painfully silent.

I bowed.

Finally, from the very back row, Nabila's parents rose and applauded loudly.

"Bravo," yelled her father. "We knew you had it in you!"

"Oh, you've made us so proud," her mother yelled. "What an amazing cultural experience."

Nabila took a big bow.

The rest of the crowd began to applaud, quietly at first. Then, slowly, they all rose and applauded loudly.

I motioned for my friends to join me on stage, and we all bowed together, poor Ben coughing the whole time. Shane gave him a sharp slap on the back and he finally stopped.

"I think we might win a Tony for this," Ben gasped.

"I think they're just happy to think it wasn't real," Gordon whispered.

"Joke's on them," said Shane. "That was real . . . right?"

"I have an idea," Nabila said. "I think that . . ."

My mother rose—like a zombie—and walked past us to the podium.

"Shhh," I said to the others. "We can talk about it later. I'm just glad we somehow survived."

"Hi, everyone," said my mother to the crowd, her voice shaking a bit. "I think we can hold off on new business until the next meeting. I can't really think straight. All in favor?"

"AYE," the entire crowd responded.

"What about the door prize?" asked one balding father.

My mother grabbed a canned ham and flung it to him, nearly knocking him over.

"It's all yours," she said.

Before Director Z could say "Thank you for coming," the crowd of concerned parents and teachers headed for the door. The Nurse escorts tried their best to walk folks out, but everyone wanted to leave as fast as possible.

"No, no, no," one mother said. "I can show myself out. I insist."

Director Z looked over at me with a concerned glance.

"Gordon," I whispered, "just run ahead and make sure no monsters are lurking on the way to the front door."

Gordon ran off, and my mother walked up to the rest of my friends and me.

"Oh, Chrissy," said my mother, "that was so real. I got really caught up in it. For a minute, I thought maybe the fish had gone bad, because I could have sworn I was seeing things . . ."

"See, I told you something was up with the fish!" added Ben.

Nabila smacked his head.

"Is this why you're always here so late at night, and so stressed?" asked my mother.

I stared at her, dumbfounded.

"Yeah," chirped Shane. "And if you think this is good, wait until you see our karate routine! We'll have it ready for you next month."

"Oh, no," my mother gasped. "That's quite all right. I'd hate to bother all the old folks. It was such a nice gesture that Director Z let us use this space, but I think we'll go back to the Rotary Dinner Hall next time."

"Aw, come on, Mrs. T," said Shane. "This was an amazing performance."

"Well," she said, "I'll think about it."

She turned to leave, still shaking a bit and mumbling to herself.

Once she left, I turned to Shane.

"What were you thinking, inviting my mother back to Gallow Manor after we barely survived this time?"

Shane replied something along the lines of "I dunno," but I could only focus on the creature that had appeared behind him.

"GWARRRRR!" growled the creature.

The Masked Avengers

"WHA!" I screamed and pointed behind Shane. "It's back!"

Shane spun around and landed in a karate pose.

"Kick its head," I called out.

Then we heard a giggle coming from underneath the horrifying face. I took a closer look to see that Nabila's body was sticking out from under the head. Her fluorescent fanny pack was unmistakable.

She pulled off the monster head and handed it to me.

"I think this is a Balinese mask," she said. "Perhaps with some sort of enchantment on it. There are similar masks in Egyptian tradition."

"It's ugly," said Ben, who grabbed the mask from my hands and sneezed again. "And heavy. Do you think this is real hair? What's up with the mirrors on the tongue?"

"I read in the *The Book of the Dead* that masks are sometimes used to protect the dead," she said.

"This place is obviously haunted," said Shane.

"By 'the dead,' you mean ghosts?" Ben asked.

"The ghosts are just trying to protect themselves?" I asked. "So they're *not* trying to kill us? I think it's time we told Director Z about the vase. We need his help figuring this out, and that's when it all started."

We found Director Z in the front foyer with Gordon.

"I've just escorted the last old parent—or should I say grandparent—out to her car," Director Z said. "She was quite shook-up, but in the end, I think I convinced her that she had just watched a bit of performance art. I think we somehow made it through the PTA meeting without letting out any of our secrets. If anything, it may have drawn their attention away from the residents."

"Director Z," I said. "I have something to tell you."

"Let me guess," he said. "You broke something."

"How did you know?" Gordon asked.

"A major blizzard formed over the manor, for one." Director Z started counting things off on his fingers. "Lucinda was screaming about evil spirits all night. There was a hole in the banquet hall door thanks to an ax. You—"

"You knew?" Nabila gasped. "Why didn't you do anything?"

"I told you that if you broke anything, you'd pay," he said. "I sensed a disgruntled nature in the spirits of this house and I could feel that they were very much upset with our presence. But I also knew that if we just kept to ourselves, and didn't bother them incessantly, they'd leave us be."

"So the house *is* haunted!" said Shane.

"Did you have any doubt after what just happened?" Ben asked.

"I had my theories," Shane replied.

"What was it?" asked Director Z. "What did you break?"

"A vase," we all said at once.

"Not the vase in the North Wing?" asked Director Z.

"That's the one," said Gordon. "Technically the werewolves broke it!"

"It doesn't matter who broke it," Director Z said. "I

believe it held the ashes of one of the matriarchs of the family. You must make peace with the spirits."

"How?" I asked.

"You're smart kids, you'll figure it out," he said. "I'd start with the North Wing. That's where this all started. That's where you should try to end it."

"Hello?" Shane yelled into the North Wing hallway. "Ghosts? We're so sorry. We didn't mean to break your vase."

"Yeah," added Gordon. "We were stupid, and we're sorry. Please stop haunting us now."

"We brought you your mask back," I said, holding up the mask as an offering.

"Come out and get it," said Ben with a sniffle.

There was silence in the North Wing hallway.

Nabila paced back and forth as we waited for some sort of reply.

"All right, I've had enough!" she yelled. "Just because we broke the vase with your old dead mother doesn't mean you have the right to kill us. She was already dead!"

An angry rumble filled the hall.

"If you have anything to say about it, come out here at ONCE!" Nabila finished with a flourish.

"What are you doing?" Ben asked. "You're just going to make them madder!"

A ghostly figure appeared in the hallway and rushed toward us, raising a short sword in the air.

"You foooools," yelled the ghost, who, as he came closer, looked terribly old. He wore a tattered old uniform.

"I care not about that dusty old vase," he said. "No ashes of a blood relative lay in it."

"Okay, so what's the problem?" asked Shane.

"Those terrible old monsters you've brought into our home," he said, moving closer to Shane, sword still raised. "They snort and snot and burp and barf. They're unclean. I don't want such filth in our house. They disgust me!"

With that, he swung his ghostly old sword at Shane's neck.

"Shane!" yelled Nabila.

It went through Shane's neck but didn't even leave a mark.

"Cool," said Shane.

"Cool?" hissed the old ghost. "I would go so far as to say that my blade is ice-cold."

"No, I meant 'cool' like 'neat' or 'awesome,'" said Shane. "What time period are you from, anyway?"

A ghostly kid appeared and ran toward us. "1897. What year is it now?"

"2014," I replied.

"Wow, I've been dead for one hundred seventeen years. That's thirteen times the amount of time I was alive."

"So you're nine," Nabila said, never failing a math quiz. "We're all eleven and twelve. What's your name?"

"I'm Quincy," he replied. "And this is my great-grandfather, George Stratford."

"That's Lieutenant Commander Stratford to you," he grumbled.

"You'll have to pardon my grandfather," said another ghost as he joined Quincy and George. "He talks so much about these old monsters that sometimes I think *he's* the old monster."

Another ghost appeared out of nowhere. A woman. And then a little girl came into view.

"That's my mother, Mary Stratford, but she likes to be called Lady Stratford," said Quincy. "And my three-year-old sister, Leila."

Five ghosts in total.

"We're so sorry we frightened you," Lady Stratford said. "But we were at our wits' end. When those werewolves destroyed the vase and left such a mess, why, we couldn't help but lash out."

"They can't stand messes," added Quincy.

"But we never would have hurt you," Quincy's father said. "We were just trying to convince you to leave this house."

"It was you in those masks?" I asked.

"Yes," said Quincy's father.

"I collected those terrifying masks from the island of Bali during a tour with the Royal Navy," said George. "They are said to channel the spirit of Rangda—an evil witch who eats small children. I thought they'd spook you out of the house good, but here you are now, standing right in front of me."

"Why are you still in the house?" Shane asked.

"We were trapped in the South Wing when the fire started," said Quincy's father. "We think it was the servants."

"But there is no South Wing," Gordon said.

"Exactly," said Quincy.

"We're sorry," I said. "But I think the old monsters are here to stay. All we can do is ask them to behave. And now that we know you're here, I'll ask them to do that."

"You might want to cover your mouth when you sneeze," said George, pointing at Ben. "It was such a powerful load of snot that it flew through my eyehole and directly into my eye."

All the ghosts shuddered.

"They hate bogies, too," said Quincy. "I once dug one out with my finger, and—"

"Quincy!" Lady Stratford scolded.

"Got it," said Ben.

Quincy waved as the mysterious figures faded away in front of us.

"Um . . . bye?" said Shane.

Mysterious Gifts

Somehow, Director Z convinced us to help out the next night. I think it was punishment for breaking the vase. After we shuffled around school like zombies for the day, we found ourselves standing at the snowy entrance to Gallow Manor once again.

But something was different.

"What's that noise?" asked Ben.

We all put our ears to the massive wooden door.

"Are the monsters . . . laughing?" Gordon said, flabbergasted.

"There's something else," said Nabila. "Scratching and whimpering. It sounds like a puppy."

She concentrated for a moment.

"And a kitten."

We rang the bell, and soon heard the sound of claws scraping down the hall and toward the door.

The door swung open, and a cute little brown puppy waddled out onto the welcome mat and started nibbling on Shane's shoes.

"Hey," Shane said, leaning down and patting the dog, "what's up, dude?"

"I thought your hearing was flawless," Gordon scolded Nabila. "Where's the kitten?"

From the feet of the Nurse who had answered the door, a small black-and-white kitten hissed at the dog.

"Friendly little thing," said Nabila. "I'm still trying to figure out why my ancestors were so in love with cats."

Shane shuffled the dog (and us) inside, and the Nurse closed the door.

"Where did these guys come from?" I asked the Nurse.

"Grigore," said the Nurse.

"Why are you back in your old uniform?" Ben asked. "Your tight uniform?"

"More comfortable," said the Nurse.

"I see," said Shane, thinking about it as the Nurse walked away.

The kitten took off down the hallway toward the East Wing. The puppy gave a sharp bark that echoed in the foyer, and chased after the kitten.

"Careful of the zombies!" I yelled at the furballs, and turned to my friends.

"They'll be eaten alive!" I said.

"I dunno," said Shane. "Everyone loves puppies and kittens."

"Exactly," said Gordon. "Sooooo tasty!"

"I wonder if Director Z knows about this yet," Nabila said.

"Let's go talk with Grigore first," I said.

We found the batty old vampire in the game room with the huge fireplace. He was talking with Grace, the most with-it of the zombies. She moaned in approval at something he said.

"Are you guys agreeing on who gets to eat them?" I asked.

"Oh, no," said Grigore. "Your mother's gift is just vonderful. We vouldn't even think of eating them."

"My mother's gift?" I asked, confused.

"The puppy and kitten," said Grigore. "It vas so nice of them to thank us for using the space."

"The puppy and kitten are from the PTA?" I asked.

"Yes," said Grigore. "They vere at the door this morning. I vas the vone who heard them scratching. They came vith a nice note."

"Oh no," said Ben. "The PTA has no idea what it's done."

"Where's the note?" I asked, not believing that my mother would send a puppy and kitten—at least not without talking to me first.

"I don't know," said Grigore. "I lost it somevhere vhile ve vere playing."

There was a bark in the hallway, and the cat rushed into the room and pounced on Ben. Ben screamed.

"Nooooo!" He grabbed the cat and tried to pull it off of himself.

"Claudine!" Grigore stood up and yelled. "Bad kitten! No, Claudine!"

"They named the cat Claudine?" Gordon asked, chuckling.

"My allergies!" Ben continued screaming as Grigore pulled the kitten off of him.

When Grigore finally got the cat off, Ben was covered in cat hair.

"Get the hair off of me!" said Ben. "Hurry! I'm gonna get hives!"

We brushed the hair off of Ben while Grigore sat down and stroked Claudine.

"Grab my inhaler, Nabila!" Ben shrieked. "Hurry!"

"I'm hurrying, I'm hurrying!" she shrieked back.

She dug around furiously in her fanny pack, and when she finally found the inhaler, she shoved it into Ben's hand.

He pulled off the cap, shoved the inhaler into his mouth . . .

. . . and stopped.

"Why aren't you using it?" I asked.

"I don't think I need it," he said. "I'm usually hacking and coughing and wheezing as soon as cat hair hits my skin, but I feel fine."

"Maybe it's one of those hypoallergenic cats?" Nabila said.

"Hypo-what?" asked Gordon.

"Cats that are less likely to trigger your allergies," Nabila said.

"AHHHH . . .

"AHHHHHHHHH . . .

"CHOOOOOO!" sneezed Grigore, and his dentures flew into the fireplace. They jumped out of the flames and chattered out into the hallway, most likely heading down to Grigore's coffin in the dungeon.

"Guess not," said Shane.

Before we could come up with any more theories, there was a scream from the hallway.

"You MONSTERS," said an otherworldly voice. "WE WILL DESTROY YOU!!!"

Cute and Cuddly
Poop Machines

The room shook violently. A chandelier fell on top of the chessboard, flinging Howie the werewolf and Jimmy the Moth Man back onto the dusty carpet.

The fire blew out in the fireplace.

A great roar thundered down the hallway.

"What is it?" asked Gordon, covering his ears.

"It's got to be—" I said.

"GHOOOOOOOOSTS!" Grigore finished.

The half dozen old monsters in the game room got up as fast as they could, knocking into one another as they shuffled around the shaking room.

"Why are you guys scared?" asked Gordon. "Didn't

Director Z tell you what was going on with our ghost friends?"

The puppy flopped into the room, frightened out of its mind, and right into Nabila's arms.

"Yip, yip, yip, yip," it barked.

"GET THAT THING OUT OF MY SIGHT!" A voice rattled our teeth, and Quincy's father floated into the room.

"Very angry ghost friends," said Gordon.

"Father! Father, stop!" Quincy yelled as he floated in after his father.

But Quincy's father didn't stop. He headed right toward Grigore.

"Noooooo!" Grigore cowered in the corner, holding the kitten tightly. "I don't even have any teeth. You vouldn't harm a helpless old vampire vith no teeth, vould you?"

"Helpless old vampire?" huffed Quincy's father. "You were the one that brought them into the house. These evil little things."

The kitten hissed from Grigore's arms as Quincy's father leaned in closer.

The puppy growled in Nabila's tight grip.

"Whoa," she said. "Settle down." She tried to calm the dog, but it bit her. "OUCH!"

She dropped the yipping puppy, and it scurried out of the room.

"Father," Quincy tried again. "Leave them alone. You're worse than Great-Grandfather."

"Yeah," I said, moving next to Quincy. "What's the big deal! It's just a puppy and a kitten!"

"Don't tell me how to act, boys!" he shouted. "I'm defending our house! Our honor. How dare they bring these creatures into our home . . ."

His ghostly face turned demonic; fangs poked out over his lips, his eyes glowed red, and he roared into Grigore's face.

"Please, sir," whimpered Grigore. "Please don't drain me of my juice. Please."

"He can't hurt you," I yelled at Grigore. "He's just upset that you're in his house and you let the dog and cat in."

"I can most certainly hurt him," hissed the demon ghost. "I will scare him until he's demented."

"Too late," Gordon said, giggling.

"Gentlemen, gentlemen," Shane said.

He moved between the quaking vampire and the upset ghost. The kitten saw the perfect moment for escape and bolted into the hallway.

"We can work this out," Shane said in his calmest Zen master voice. He turned to Quincy's father with his hands up in surrender.

"I know that you're upset . . . um . . . ," he said, "what's your name?"

"RICHARD," roared the ghost.

"And you have every right to let your feelings be known, Richard," Shane said calmly. "But I'd ask that you calm down just a little, otherwise Grigore will only hear that you're screaming, not that you're saying something."

Richard roared again, this time blowing Shane's hair back.

"Okay, thank you for listening," Shane said calmly, and then turned to me.

"Richard, we didn't have time to tell the monsters about you," I said. "I'm sorry. But we were pretty tired yesterday, thanks to your big show at the PTA meeting."

"That was fun," squealed Quincy.

"Har, har, har," said Ben.

"Grigore," I said, "go find Claudine and Sir Kibblebreath. I'll have to bring them back to my mother—if it really was the PTA that brought them into the house. They can't stay here—not if you want to live in this place without being haunted every day."

Grigore slowly limped out of the room, and Richard didn't stop him. The other old monsters followed, Grace the zombie taking a swipe at Richard's face with an upset groan. His face returned to normal. Well, normal for a ghost, anyway.

"Now wait a minute," Lt. Commander Stratford said as he floated into the room. "I don't think we should be too hasty, Grandson."

"Do you really want those beasts strutting around this house?" asked Richard. "You said yourself these old monsters would rain ruin upon our house—letting those terrible creatures into it is certainly a step toward that."

"I think, Grandson," Lt. Commander Stratford said, waving his short sword around the room, "that those beasts will end up doing more harm to the old monsters then they will to us, or our house."

"What do you mean?" I said.

"Oh, I don't know," said the old ghost. "I just think they've got something in them."

"Yes, they've certainly got a lot in them," said Lady Stratford as she entered the room, Leila in tow. "And quite a lot of it has come out onto our carpets. Disgusting."

The puppy and kitten scampered into the room again, and Quincy backed away.

"I think they're scary," said Quincy. "And they make my nose feel funny."

Just thinking about it, Quincy sneezed, and snorted up a huge, glowing booger. He went to pick it, when—

"Quincy!" his mother screeched. "WHAT IN HEAVENS ARE YOU DOING?"

"Ma," said Quincy. "Why are you always ruining my fun?"

"Fiddlesticks," said his mother. "You should really

use a handkerchief! It's completely uncouth."

"This is what's going to happen," I said, scooping up the dog. "We're going to get these guys out of your hair. Then, we'll introduce you to the Director, and you guys can set some ground rules about the old monsters in the house. Everyone's gonna be happy, I swear it. Shane, grab the cat."

"It was a terrible idea, anyway," added Ben. "Quincy, let me get a look at that booger . . ."

"I'll search the house for stained carpets, and do what I can to scrub up the mess," Gordon said.

"Great," I said. "Nabila, could you help Gordon?"

Nabila sat in a chair staring off into space. A long string of drool hung from her mouth.

Nothing to Sneeze At

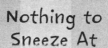

"NABILA!" screeched Ben. "What's going on?"

"It bit me," she mumbled. "So badly."

"What?" I asked.

We all rushed over. Her hand was red and swollen.

"She's having an allergic reaction to the dog bite," said Ben, and he unzipped Nabila's fanny pack. "I just need to get my rash cream, Nabila. And an allergy pill."

The Lt. Commander floated over. "See, I told you that there was something special about these mangy little furballs," he said.

I looked down at Sir Kibblebreath, and wondered if there was something special about him. He shook his little head in my arms, and some hair floated up into my nose.

"Ah, ahhhh, ahhhhhhh . . . CHOOOOO!" I sneezed so hard that the glass on the fallen chandelier shook a bit.

"Yes," said Richard. "There is something 'special' about these animals. Which is exactly why we need to get them out of our home immediately. They're making me itchy just looking at them."

"We'll leave you to help out your friend," said the Lt. Commander. "We'll be back for an update. Unless we see your friend first."

"See our friend first?" Gordon asked.

"Oh, you mean if she dies?" Shane asked.

"Exactly," wheezed the old ghost.

"Great-Grandfather!" squeaked Quincy. "You're so mean!!!"

"I'm. Not. Goingtodie." Nabila gasped. "Feeling better . . . already."

"Come on, Grandfather," said Richard. "They've had enough." Richard sneezed himself out of the room with a huge ACHOOO.

"And so have I," came Richard's voice from the hallway.

"Where do they go, anyway?" I asked as the rest of the family floated into the hall, some through the open door, and some through the walls.

Shane sneezed.

"What the heck is going on?" Ben said. "I'm feeling better than I have in weeks, and everyone else is sneezing or having allergy attacks—even the ghosts!"

"Okay, everyvone," Grigore said as he entered the room with a basket. "I've found vone of our furry little friends."

"Wait, what?" I asked. "We've already got Claudine *and* Sir Kibblebreath."

"Huh . . . ," Grigore said as he put down the basket. "But . . ."

We all peered into the basket to see . . .

Another kitten!

"What the . . ." Gordon was astonished.

Grigore sneezed, his dentureless lips flapping like a whoopee cushion.

"Were there two kittens when they arrived?" I asked Grigore.

"No," he said. "Just vone. Of each. Two in total."

Grigore scratched his bald head, trying to figure it all out.

"Are you sure?" I asked.

"Gentlemen," said Director Z as he stormed into the room. "Are you responsible for the puppy which is currently in my office?"

"Nope," said Shane. "We're just responsible for this one."

"That one looks exactly like him," said Director Z, pointing at the puppy in my arms. "Yes, that's the one. How did you get him out of my office? I just locked him in there so he wouldn't be eaten by the residents."

"So there must be two of each," I replied.

"What?" asked Director Z, annoyed. "Please tell me what's going on here. I don't think it wise to have animals at this facility."

"We're not sure what's going on," said Shane, "except that Grigore found a puppy and kitten at the door, with a thank-you note from the PTA. And he brought them in."

"Just two, though, I svear!" Grigore said.

"But then how are there four animals now, Grigore?" demanded Director Z.

"I don't know," whined Grigore.

"De. Mented," chirped Gordon.

"Stop it," Ben said, and kicked Gordon in the shin.

"Yeah, you show him," said Nabila.

"Feeling better?" I asked Nabila.

"What happened to Nabila?" asked Director Z.

"That little beast bit me," said Nabila, pointing at the puppy. "And I had a very bizarre allergic reaction."

"We'll have the witches take a look at that," said Director Z. "Or would you like Leech Lady to take a little blood from the wound?"

"I'll go see the witches," said Nabila, and she made her way out of the room.

"Chris, I need you to get these animals out of the house at once," Director Z said.

"Okay," I said. "I'll tell my mother she needs to pick me up early. Maybe we can take them back where she got them. Shane, can you help?"

"Sure thing," said Shane. "The sooner the better. I'm starting to get hives."

"Gordon and Ben," said Director Z, "can you please help the chefs prepare dinner? It's taco night, so things might get messy, between the olives, onions, eye-of-newt, and other toppings crawling all over the place."

Director Z, Shane, and I were left alone.

"You swear you didn't have anything to do with this?" he asked.

"Why would I?" I replied. "Feeding baby animals to old monsters is just not a hobby of mine."

"Have you had a chance to speak with the ghosts?" asked Director Z.

"Yeah, and we were able to chill them out, until the puppy and kitten showed up," Shane said.

"That old ghost loves the animals for some reason," I said. "Do you think he brought them?"

"I'm not sure," said Director Z, "but I don't like them. They—"

Director Z stopped and quickly pulled out a handkerchief.

"Don't like who?" asked Shane.

Director Z paused with the handkerchief in front of his nose.

"I think he means the puppies and kittens," I said.

"AAAAAAACHOOOOO!" Director Z sneezed. "Get them out of here, boys."

When she picked me up, my mother confirmed that she hadn't sent any pets to the retirement home.

"Although that does sound like a good idea," she said. "I wish I had thought of it. I hear animals really help old people stuck in retirement homes feel happy."

I wondered for a moment if Grigore was lying about where the puppy and kitten came from, but didn't think about it long. They'd have a new home soon.

Luckily, my mom's friend Barbara runs a rescue shelter. As we drove there, Shane and I tried to contain the animals as they raced around the inside of the car.

"WHHHHAAAAAACHOOOO!" I sneezed.

A huge wad of green snot broke into booger chunks on the windshield. It looked like a bird had eaten split pea soup and relieved itself on our car.

My mother turned on the windshield wipers with an EWWWWW.

"No, Mom," I said with a snort. "That's on the inside."

"WELL, COVER YOUR NOSE NEXT TIME," she screeched as my boogers dripped onto the dashboard.

Lunch Lady
Liaisons

Ben and I were sitting in Mr. Bradley's social studies class when I *thought* I saw someone's face in the door window, staring right at me.

I couldn't be sure. I was still suffering from the aftereffects of being trapped in the car with the cats and dogs the day before, and was feeling a little foggy. The good news—I couldn't smell Mr. Bradley's breath today.

My nose dripped all over my Social Studies book. I was running out of tissues and I had given up trying to catch every bit of nose ooze.

"Looks like you've flooded the Great Wall of China," Ben said, pointing at the open chapter on Chinese culture. "I thought that was impossible."

"I can't even think straight right now," I said.

The door to the classroom opened up, and Lunch Lady poked her head into the room.

"Meester Bradley?" she said.

"What do you want, Ms. Veracruz?" asked Mr. Bradley.

"I want those two boys," she said, pointing at Ben and me. "They have to answer for the chicken casserole all over my cash register."

Ben looked at me strangely, but we knew not to say anything.

"Why doesn't the principal have a word with them?" Mr. Bradley asked, confused.

"Oh, that's where I'm breengeeng them," said Lunch Lady. "Right to thee principal."

"All right," said Mr. Bradley.

Lunch Lady quickly pulled us out of the classroom and rushed us down the hall into the janitor's closet.

As she closed the door behind us, I said, "You can't just pull us out of class like that."

"Actually, you can pull us out of Mr. Bradley's class any time," said Ben. "His breath is the worst. Though the barf water in the janitor's mop bucket comes in a close second."

"What if Bradley checks in with Principal Prouty?" I asked.

"He's too lazy to check my story," said Lunch Lady. "And this is *muy serio.*"

"What if the janitor shows up for a mop?" I asked.

"I gave heem some cheecken Parmesan to eat—hees favorite," Lunch Lady sighed, and then quickly snapped back to attention. "If you're worried about thee janeetor, shut up and leesten!"

"Okay, okay," I said. "What is it!?"

"There are more aneemals running around Gallow Manor," said Lunch Lady. "A lot more! The Director has geeven me thees letter to geeve to you." She held it up. "You are to get your friends, give eet to thee principal, and hope she dismeesses you early for thee day."

"What does it say?" Ben asked and went to tear open the letter.

"Don't touch eet!" said Lunch Lady, smacking Ben's hand. "Eet has to look official."

"Please tell me it doesn't have a glowing signature," I said.

"Just geet your friends, and geet the letter to thee principal," growled Lunch Lady.

It was 2:00 and we found ourselves lined up in the principal's office.

"From what I hear around school," Nabila said, "only bad kids end up in the principal's office. I don't like this."

Principal Prouty sat at her desk, eyeing the crusty old letter, which she had taken out of the sealed envelope. The smell of mold filled the room.

Shane sneezed. Gordon tried to stop his nose from snotting.

"Those poor creatures," Principal Prouty mumbled as she read the letter.

She put the letter down and stared at me.

"Sooooo . . . ," I said nervously.

"Well," said Principal Prouty. "You have to go help them with the outbreak. Zachary says it's pretty bad."

"Yesssss . . . ," I said, wondering what exactly Director Z had told the principal.

"So, you know Zachary?" asked Shane. "I mean, the Director?"

"We have an ongoing business relationship, yes," said Principal Prouty simply.

She stared at us.

We stared back.

Nabila finally broke the silence.

"All right!" she chirped. "Let's get out of here, then!"

We all stumbled awkwardly out of Principal Prouty's

office, like we were spooked old monsters and she was an angry ghost.

My mother reluctantly drove us to Gallow Manor. It took a bit to convince her that Director Z had arranged some of during-school-hours volunteering with the principal.

As the sound of her car faded into the distance, we could hear strange new sounds coming from the manor.

BRRRRAAAACK.

SLLLLUUUUUURRROOONT.

HAAAAAAA-CHOOOO!

WAAAAAAAAAAA!

"They're all sick!" said Nabila.

The door swung in to reveal a very sick-looking Nurse. He sneezed in our faces with a spray of boogers and then passed out. His head hit the mat outside of the door with a thud.

"Nurse Ax?" I yelled, getting down to check on him.

"Nurse Ax?" Shane slapped his cheeks.

"Are you sure that isn't Nurse Inx?" said Ben.

"Nurse? Nurse?"

We were all bent over the Nurse when another

figure appeared in the doorway. The even-gaunter, even-whiter figure of Director Z. He looked insanely sick. He stared at us with his red eyes, loosening his always-perfect tie. He swayed in the doorway, about to collapse.

"Children," he said. "Help."

Nothing to Sniff At

"Director Z!" I screamed.

Shane and I rushed up to him to make sure he didn't fall.

"Don't forget about me," said the Nurse, but his face was smashed on the welcome mat, so it came out, "Don forgt ba me."

"Yes, yes," said Director Z, "I'm fine. I just got dizzy. Help Nurse Ax out."

Gordon and Shane bent to pick up Nurse Ax, and with a huge grunt from all three of them, he was back on his feet again.

"What's going on?" asked Nabila.

Director Z opened the door wider, and presented

the foyer with a flourish.

Inside, dozens of puppies and kittens were running around like crazy. Up to the North Wing. From the West Wing.

In the East Wing, Lucinda B. Smythe screeched, "Oh, heavens, there's just so many of them!"

"There are *too* many of them," said Director Z. "Just when we think we've cornered them all in one room, a monster screams from another part of the manor."

"Scream?" Gordon asked. "Why would the monsters be afraid of them?"

"I think the sheer numbers," said Director Z, "and the fact that they're multiplying so fast may have something to do with it. Not to mention, I've never been more allergic to a creature in my life."

Director Z sneezed so hard that snot flew through the fingers of the hand he had placed over his mouth.

"I hear that," I said, and my nose started to twitch. "This place is swarming with fur."

"I have something to show you," he said, and beckoned us down the West Wing hallway.

"They're everywhere," said Ben as we made our way to the werewolves' room.

"Kittens swatting at each other," Shane said. "Puppies rolling over one another. Normally I love this stuff—when the puppies and kittens aren't multiplying like freaky amoebas."

"Clearly something unnatural is happening," said Nabila as we entered the bedroom.

"Clearly," said Director Z, pointing at a curled-up old dog on a chewed-up mattress.

"Who is it?" I gasped.

"It's Howie," said Director Z sadly. "And he's suffered a severe monster juice drainage. He passed out here after peeing all over the harpsichord. Did you know that before he played accordion, he played the harpsichord? It must have been the only thing he recognized in this place. So sad."

Director Z looked tired and zoned out.

"The puppies and kittens did this to him?" asked Gordon.

Howie's leg twitched, and Nabila bent down to stroke it.

"It's okay," she said. "It's just a bad dream."

A banshee screamed past the open door to Howie's room, chased by a half dozen dogs.

"This is no dream," Director Z snapped, regaining some of his energy. "The puppies and kittens did do this to him, and I'm still trying to figure out how. But a few of the residents and I have come up with a theory.

"These animals give off toxic allergens—that much we know. Even for us, the living, they have an effect."

"AAAAACHOO," Gordon sneezed. "Yep."

Gordon turned to Ben.

"Dude, I'm sorry I made fun of you for your allergies," Gordon said. "This totally bites."

"But I believe that, with the residents, the allergies are actually something worse," continued Director Z. "Something far, far worse. I believe that the puppies and kittens are absorbing monster juice. They get their victims ill, and then, when their monster juice escapes, they're there to absorb it. Not by biting, or eating, just by . . . being in the area."

"Little monster juice sponges," said Shane.

"Once they have too much monster juice to handle, they split in two—or three or four, who knows—and they absorb even more. My guess is there were a few more kittens and puppies in the manor last night when you took the first four away with your mother. There are so many places to hide in this massive manor. The dungeon alone . . ."

"Let's talk with the ghosts," I said. "They'd probably be able to float easily through the house and see into places where we can't see. We'll need their help to get all of them out of here."

"No, we have to keep them here," said Director Z. "They're too ordinary-looking. If we turned them out into the wild, they might find owners, and who knows what else they're capable of."

"Oh no!" Nabila said. "What about the kittens and puppies at the animal shelter?"

"I don't think we need to worry about that for the moment," said Director Z. "They barely had any exposure to the monster juice here, and there's no monster juice present at the shelter—at least none that I know of—so they should remain weak. We must first focus on the issue at hand."

"What if we just . . . ," Gordon said, and motioned cutting his throat with his thumb.

"Gordon!" Shane gasped.

"I thought about that," said Director Z, "but again, they might not die if killed. They might grow stronger. No. We need to gather them all into one room. And, Shane, you have to stop seeing them as cute little cuddly-wuddlies and realize that they are the new threat to monsterdom!"

"Man, this is just so sad," said Shane.

"We need to work quickly!" said Director Z. "Luckily, we aren't filled with monster juice to drain, but we can get sick, and if we have severe allergic reactions, we could all die. The Nurses and I have already been exposed too much. I need you gentlemen and lady to set things in motion while my staff and I walk the grounds and try to air out our sinuses. First things first. Talk with the ghosts."

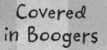

Covered in Boogers

"Ha-ha-haaaa!" Lt. Commander Stratford's chuckle filled the North Wing hallway. "You want us to help YOU! I'm having too much fun watching those old monsters suffer. I haven't been this happy since my dear sister was still with me."

The old Lt. Commander stood atop a small spiral staircase that led to a number of small rooms on the second floor, as well as the balcony that surrounded the wing.

"You nasty old fart!" Gordon yelled up the staircase. "No wonder your sister ran away. Where are the nice ghosts? I want to talk with the nice ghosts!"

"She didn't *leave* me," he said. "She was a ghost like

me, but her energies were drained and I lost her. I'd do anything to get her back. And I'd do anything to get rid of those old monsters."

Quincy, Leila, and their parents slowly materialized next to Lt. Commander Stratford.

"Teeheehee," said Quincy. "Great-Grandfather, you just got called an old fart!"

"I disagree, Grandfather," said Richard. "I'd do anything to get rid of those nasty animals. We must help these children.

"And, in return"—Richard pointed a ghostly finger directly at my head—"you WILL get the old monsters to behave. And they will stay away from the North Wing. And we will stay away from them. Agreed?"

"Agreed," we all said.

"Poppycock!" yelled the old ghost as he raised his sword. "My family might have an agreement with you, but I, most certainly, do NOT. CHAAAARGE!"

He floated swiftly down the stairway, sword pointed at our heads.

"I really wish he'd stop doing this," said Gordon.

"I think it feels pretty cool," said Shane.

WHOOOOSH!

With a roar, the old ghost shot through our bodies and into a supply closet at the bottom of the stairs.

"Dreadfully sorry about that," said Richard. "He always has to make a point."

The closet door shot open and a dozen puppies and kittens tumbled out with the old ghost, who was coughing and hacking and moving much slower now.

"Can't. BREATHE," he wheezed. "Get. Them. Away!"

"Ghosts breathe?" asked Nabila.

George slowly floated up the staircase.

"Well, don't bring them up here!" said Lady Stratford.

But, before the ghosts could float away, they began coughing and sneezing as the animals, and all of their dander, came floating up the stairs with the old Lt. Commander.

"Great. Grand. Father," coughed Quincy. "Are. You. Okay?"

The puppies and kittens jumped around inside the forms of the ghosts, which were frozen at the top of the stairs.

"Guys! Guys!" yelled Ben. "Are you okay?"

HACK, COUGH, SNORT!

"We've got to get the puppies and kittens away from them," I said, and we rushed up the stairs.

Halfway up, each ghost, in unison, leaned back with an "AAAAAHHHH . . .

"AHHHHHHHHHHHH . . .

"CHOOOOOOOOOOO!"

A shower of glowing, emerald-green snot—filled

with boogery chunks—showered down on us from the top of the stairs, pouring out of each of the ghosts.

We slipped and stumbled backward, falling down the stairs with the animals, which had all been thrown down with us.

When I finally was able to get up out of the muck, I realized I couldn't hear out of my right ear. I pulled a huge booger out of my ear hole.

"Oh man!" I yelled, looking down. "This is disgusting."

"Well, the good news is, I feel much better," said Quincy. "Whew, that felt great! How about you guys?"

The other ghosts nodded.

"And we've got a good batch of animals," said Shane.

"All right, everyone, grab 'em, I guess!" I said.

"I need to take a quick shower," said Ben. "I'm sort of grossed way out over here."

"We don't have time," I said. "We've got to move fast—monsters are getting sick."

"We'll float around the house and let you know where we find them," Richard said.

It was a long, hard afternoon of animal wrangling that had turned into a rougher evening. We stood snotting and wheezing in front of the banquet hall, which was filled with nearly fifty puppies and kittens.

SNORF!

SNORRRRT!

SNAAAARRRRF!

"I feel like my clothes are turning into armor with all of these drying boogers," said Gordon.

"All of the animal hair doesn't help, either," said Shane. "It just sticks right on. AHHHHCHOOO!"

A Shane booger hit my temple.

"Ugggggggh," I grunted, and wiped off the fresh, hot booger.

"Ack!" yelled Nabila. "You tossed it right at me."

She in turn tossed the hot booger, and—

"How dare you!" yelled Lucinda B. Smythe.

Shane's booger sat on her portrait in a way that made her look like she had lost a tooth.

"Wow, she looks like a hockey player," said Gordon, laughing.

"That's *not* funny," said Lucinda.

Quincy floated up behind Nabila and leaned in close to her.

"PSSSSST," whispered Quincy.

"Wahhhhh!" screamed Nabila. "AAAHHHCHOOO!"

"I scared a sneeze out of you," Quincy said, giggling.

"It's better than a fart." Gordon snickered. "AAAACHOO!"

"Sorry, I couldn't help it." Quincy kept giggling. "I just came to tell you that we can't see any puppies or kittens hiding anywhere."

"Yeah, well how do you like this?" asked Nabila.

She pulled a crusty chunk of boogery hair off of her shirt and tossed it at Quincy. It hit his head and floated around a bit.

"Ah, ah, ahhhhh . . . " Quincy shook his head. "SCHPLOOOOOOO!"

Quincy shot up through the ceiling, showering emerald-green boogers down on us and Lucinda—now it looked like she had lost several teeth.

"EEEEEWWWWWWW," we all said.

A door to one of the empty rooms in the East Wing swung open, and Murrayhotep stuck his head out. He eyed us through his wrappings.

"Would you cretins please shut up?" he growled. "I'm concentrating in here."

SLAM!

"Well, it looks like the monsters feel better already," said Shane. "At least that monstrous old monster."

"Well, then, I think we're finally done. Even if we're not done, we're done," I said, exhausted. "I'm done. Are you guys done? It's the Nurses' turn."

As we walked to the foyer, a sick zombie collapsed

in front of us. A froth of snot bubbled up through his mouth and nose, and he spasmed violently on the floor.

"We've got to get him to a Nurse," said Nabila as she bent over to pick him up.

We saw more sick monsters as we dragged the zombie through the foyer.

"Clarice, you don't need to use that anymore," I said, pointing at her walker. "It's gonna be a while before my mother comes back for another visit if she ever comes back."

"But I actually need it now," she wheezed.

We passed the zombie off to a Nurse and headed for Director Z's office in the West Wing. There was moaning and groaning like we hadn't heard since the days of Raven Hill.

We passed by Old Bigfoot's room on the way to Director Z's office.

"Help," he screamed and coughed. "Helllllp!"

I grabbed the door handle.

"It's locked," I said. "Gordon?"

"Got it," he said, and busted the door open with his shoulder.

Inside there was a pitiful sight.

"He's been pinned to his bed," Nabila said, pointing, "by a kitten?"

Shane snatched the kitten off of the beastly, hairy man, whose snow-white fur—which had been gray just a few days ago—was a devastated war zone of snot around his neck.

"You look terrible, Roy," said Shane. "How long has this been going on?"

"I don't know." Roy shook and coughed. "I woke up with it on my chest. ON MY CHEST. WHAAAAA-CHOOO!"

We were once again showered in boogers.

"I'll rush this one to the banquet hall," said Shane.

There was a loud POP, and Shane suddenly was holding two kittens.

They both looked up at him with a "mew."

"I mean I'll rush *these* to the banquet hall," said Shane. "I'll ask Murrayhotep what his secret is—he's the only one doing okay right now!"

"WHAAAACHOOO"—Shane sneezed his way down the hall.

"I feel terrible," Roy said. "Get. Me. A. Nurssppplloorrfff!" Roy began to choke on his own snot, writhing around in the bed for a moment, and then going deathly still.

"Roy!" I screeched. "Roy!"

Gordon put his ear down to Roy's twisted mouth.

"Get a Nurse!" yelled Gordon. "He's barely breathing!"

Ben snagged a Nurse from the hallway, and the Nurse ordered us out.

"What's going to happen to him?" asked Nabila as the Nurse slammed the door in our faces.

The SLAM echoed through my swollen head.

"My head!" I yelled. "It's bursting with snot."

"My mother just texted to say I could stay later," said Ben. "I feel great, and Director Z and the Nurses could use my help. You guys get out of here. Get some rest, or you'll end up like Roy. I'll let Director Z know."

Later that night I sat up in bed. No matter what position I tried, I couldn't keep myself from feeling like I was drowning in snot. I grabbed my phone off of the nightstand and texted Ben.

How are things going?

Not good. But I have an amazing idea.

What is it?

We need to get a monster to eat boogers. Ghost boogers.

Ghost Boogers
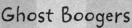

The next day at lunch, Gordon, Shane, Nabila, and I sat with tissues shoved up our noses to stop the snotting. We forced down our lunches. I had spent the morning either snotting, or trying desperately to not fall asleep.

"The monsters aren't getting much better," said Ben. "Roy's still in a coma. Lots of them were even older-looking than when you left."

Ben stopped to chomp down on a Grilled Scream and shoved a handful of French Flies into his mouth.

"I feel bad for the monsters, but oh, man, this is the most I've tasted in months," he said, energized.

"Good for you," grunted Gordon. His eyes were crusted shut and his nose was practically raw from blowing it so much. "I had to skip practice this morning. I can already feel my muscles shrinking."

Some kid tried to sit down at the end of our table, so Nabila pulled the tissue out of one of her nostrils. After a small shower of snot landed on the table, the kid walked away.

"Aw, thanks," said Ben. "I just really don't feel like barfing today."

"So, tell me again about the ghost boogers," said Shane.

"Wait," I snorted. "You were for real last night? I thought you were joking."

"No, I think it might actually work," said Ben. "Director Z is waiting for some 'removal crew' to come in from the Canadian retirement home network and take away the cats and dogs, but things are still so bad—leftover allergens and stuff—that he was thinking about moving the old folks."

He shoved another handful of greasy French Flies into his mouth.

"Careful, dude," said Shane. "You'll spew."

"Naw, not today," Ben said. "Anyway, I had a flash of inspiration. I was feeling so good, I realized that my body had somehow formed an immunity to whatever it was the puppies and kittens were exposing us to."

"What does that have to do with ghost boogers?" Nabila asked.

"Like me, they aren't as affected by the puppies and kittens. Except for when they're overexposed. Then they explode in snot. But I think it's some sort of ghostly immunity defense."

"So you're saying eating the boogers would make the monsters immune, too?" asked Shane. "Like a vaccine."

"Like the way vaccines are made from the viruses they fight?" I asked.

"Maybe, and yes," said Ben. "I think it might power them up for a bit—not necessarily cure them. I told Director Z, and he agreed—if one of us tested it."

"You mean we have to eat boogers?" asked Gordon.

"Well, one of you guys needs to, since I'm not sick. He's worried that if we test it on a monster and it backfires, it could really do some damage," said Ben. "And he can't test it, because he can't be knocked out with an allergy attack."

"What about a Nurse?" asked Nabila.

"Same thing," said Ben. "They're just too important. Look, it's just a handful of boogers. If it works—awesome—we have a whole staircase of snot to chisel off and pass around to the old monsters. If it doesn't, I'll be standing by with my inhaler, creams . . . all sorts of stuff."

We reluctantly headed to Gallow Manor after school to test Ben's theory. None of us were too excited about the idea of eating boogers. We all knew it had to be done, but no one—other than Ben—was looking forward to it.

As we entered the East Wing, the smell of the puppies and kittens coming from the banquet hall was overwhelming.

"AHHH-AHHH . . ." I struggled with a sneeze.

"CHOOOOO!" Nabila finished my sentence.

"This is bad," Gordon said with a snort. "But I feel like eating ghost boogers is going to be worse."

"Oh, finally," said Lucinda as we stepped in front of her boogered face. "It took you a full day, but you're finally back to clean me up."

"Well, we'll start with one," said Ben. "And then we'll see what happens."

"You do it," said Gordon to Shane.

"No, I think our fearless leader should do it," said Shane. "Chris, lead by example."

"If this works, you're all going to be eating boogers," Ben said. "So—just do it!"

"Fine," said Nabila, and she reached up to the portrait to pluck off the biggest booger.

"Make sure it's not mine," said Shane. "The one you flung, remember?"

"It's not yours," said Nabila, and she stared at her snack. "Okay. Here we go. I'm doing it."

She plopped it into her mouth.

The sound of Gordon dry-heaving beside me only made the situation worse. There was no way I was going to be able to do this.

"Dear child, what are you doing?" screeched Lucinda.

"I'd suggest chewing on it," said Ben. "You know, grind it up good."

Nabila took Ben's advice, gritted her teeth, and started to chew.

CRUNCH, CRUNCH, CRUNCH.

"Sounds dry," said Shane.

"Uggghhh," Nabila said through her closed mouth.

Her eyes started to water. A little sweat formed on her forehead.

CRUNCH, SQUISH, SQUISH.

A trickle of green drool dribbled down her chin.

"That's good," coached Ben. "Just like that. Now swallow."

Nabila swallowed hard . . .

GULP!

. . . and turned a boogery-green color.

"Oh no. Oh man," she said. "Whuuuurp!"

She gagged.

"You have to keep it down," said Ben. "Keep it down."

"Huhhhhhh." She dry-heaved a little but nothing

came up. "Okay. I'm okay."

Then she took in a huge breath of air through her cleared nasal passages.

"Yes! It works!" screamed Ben, giving Nabila an awkward bear hug.

Gordon, Shane, and I looked at each other. We knew what had to happen next.

"Perhaps being sick isn't so bad," said Gordon. "Maybe I don't need to play sports or be fit."

"Just do it," said Ben. "It isn't so bad, right, Nabila?"

"Isn't so bad? I just ate a giant booger," she replied. "It was disgusting. But I do feel much better."

Shane plucked a booger off of Lucinda.

"Looks like we might clean you off yet," he said.

"Well, hurry it up," said Lucinda.

"Mmmmm," Shane said as he popped it into his mouth, though his eyes said, "Blarrrf!"

I peeled more boogers off and handed some to Gordon, who reluctantly took them from me.

"Good luck," I said, and chomped down on a handful of boogers.

Gordon slowly pushed his boogers past his lips and into his mouth.

We choked down our snot snack and breathed deeply for the first time in days.

"Wahooo!" Shane yelled. "Let's grab a few green ones and feed them to an old monster."

We rushed back to the West Wing and Director Z's office with a good handful of boogers.

When we got to his office, Pietro was there, talking about the flea infestation that had come along with the puppies and kittens.

"We're sick *and* we're itching like crazy," Pietro said, a large string of snot falling out of his nose.

Even though he was in human form, he took off his shoe and started to scratch behind his ears with his foot.

"How'd you like to feel better?" asked Shane.

I held out my hand to Pietro.

"It worked?" asked Director Z.

"Sure did," said Ben.

"What is it?" asked Pietro.

Nabila replied, "They're boo—"

"Bound to make you feel better," I cut Nabila off. "Just eat it."

Pietro crunched and munched on his treat, and swallowed hard. "Ewww . . . what is this stuff?"

"We'll tell you, but first tell us, how do you feel?" asked Ben.

"Pretty good, actually," he said, and then breathed in deeply.

"Hoooooooooooowl," Pietro said, rattling the windows in Director Z's office. "Wow, I feel really good."

He stood up and stretched.

"He's still gray and wrinkly, but he looks good," said Nabila.

"He would probably just have to eat more to get more energy back," Ben said.

"Eat more what?" asked Pietro.

"Boogers," said Director Z. "Ghost boogers. Amazing."

"Ghost boogers?" Pietro gagged. "Is this a joke?"

"You feel great, right?" I asked.

"Yeah, I suppose," said Pietro. "Just a little disgusted."

"Awesome," I said. "Then maybe you could help us collect all of the boogers in the North Wing that the ghosts left behind."

"I'll get the old monsters prepared," said Director Z.

Pietro stared at the stairs, scratching his bushy werewolf-hair head.

"Boogers?" he asked. "What boogers? I don't see any boogers."

"I don't, either," said Ben.

"The stairs are now the cleanest part of the house,"

said Shane. "They almost sparkle."

He put down his rusty metal booger-collecting pail that Director Z and the Nurses had scrounged up for each of us, and called out, "Quincy! Quincy!"

"Hey, guys!" Quincy appeared at the top of the stairs. "Don't the stairs look great?"

"Ghosts can clean?" Nabila asked. "Why was this place so dusty when we first got here?"

"I told you that my parents hated bogies," Quincy said. "As soon as you guys left, we cleaned it all up. Why are you so upset?"

"Believe it or not, we think that your boogers are the key to saving the old monsters from the effects of the puppies and kittens," I said.

"Oh . . ." Quincy thought about it for a minute. "Well here, then."

Quincy dug into his ghost nose with his ghost finger and pulled out some green gold. He handed it to Pietro.

"Thanks, kid," he said over a boogery crunch.

"But I think we're going to need a lot more than that," Ben said, and held up his bucket. "Buckets and buckets."

We all held up our buckets.

"Quincy," I said, "you and your family have to help us. You need to fill these buckets for us."

"Impossible," said Lady Stratford, who materialized suddenly to his right. "You ask too much of my family. We just want peace."

I was about to plead our case, when Quincy did it for me.

"Mom," said Quincy, "if we don't help the old monsters, they'll just get older. And louder. And dirtier. It will just be worse for us."

The rest of the family appeared at the top of the stairs.

"Plus—remember when you and Dad were worried about who was going to move in here? Well, these old monsters don't even care we're here. In fact, we can float about freely. If a stuffy old rich family moved in here, we'd have to hide."

"I guess you're right . . . ," said Lady Stratford.

"You're not really thinking of forcing yourself to sneeze like you did before, are you?" Richard said.

"We have no choice, dear," Lady Stratford said. "Your son is right. He's sharp as a tack, just like his father."

"Fiddlesticks," said the Lt. Commander. "They can all go to—"

"Grandfather!!" everyone screamed.

"Okay," said Richard. "What do we need to do?"

Buckets of Boogers

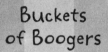

Once again we stood in front of the door to the banquet hall—this time with the ghosts.

"Will someone *please* finish cleaning this mess off of me?" screeched Lucinda B. Smythe.

"Free boogers!" said Gordon. "Go for it, Pietro."

Pietro walked over to the portrait and began to lick the remaining boogers off of Lucinda.

"Oh. Stop. No," said Lucinda. "Not like this. Ack! Your breath is terrible. Be careful! I'm an OIL painting!"

"Hey, who was it that hacked into the door with the ax?" asked Ben.

"I'm loath to admit it, but that was me," said Richard.

"Well, we have the perfect tool now," said Ben. "You

can stick your head into the banquet hall through the ax hole to soak up all the animal dander you need and then one of us will be holding on to a bucket for you."

"We're ghosts, son. A locked door is no problem for us," Richard said as he shoved his ghost head through the door.

I stood steady with my bucket.

"AHHHHHHH . . ."

The butt cheeks in his fincly pressed pants raised up once.

"AHHHHHHHHHHHHH . . ."

Twice.

"AHHHHHHHHHHHHHHHHHHH . . ."

He pulled his head out from the door and aimed for my bucket with bug eyes.

"CHOOOOOOSHLURBSCHLURBSCHLURP!"

His ghost nostrils flared, his lips flapped, and out poured the snot.

And he kept going!

"My bucket's almost full," I yelled. "Shane!"

Shane pushed his bucket above mine, and Richard filled it halfway up.

"Yeah!" said Ben. "Awesome. Nice snottin'!"

Lady Stratford was next, followed by Quincy. We were up to four buckets.

"I don't think we need to force any snot out of Leila," I said.

But she walked over to the bucket Quincy had just filled, dug deep into her little ghost nose, and picked out a surprisingly large booger.

"Bogie for you," the little three-year-old said with a smile.

"Oh, Leila, how sweet!" cooed her mother. "That's so nice of you."

"Nice," said Quincy, and he dug into his nose.

"Tut-tut." His mother slapped his ghost finger out of his nose. "That's enough for now."

We headed into the dining room of the West Wing, where Director Z and the Nurses had gathered every resident.

HAAAAACHOOO!

GWAAARRRFFF!

SNOOOORRFFFF!

Everyone in the room was sick. The table was covered in a layer of monster snot, and with each AHCHOO the layer got thicker. In some places, it dripped off of the tables.

"They're so much older than before," said Nabila.

"I can't take it!" screeched Griselda. "I'm itching everywhere. The *inside* of my body itches." Griselda fell to the floor, writhing in agony. She began choking, and a Nurse swiftly pulled her up and slapped her on the back.

Murrayhotep leaned back in his chair, giggling.

"Why is Murrayhotep so happy?" asked Ben. "Why isn't he sick?"

Before anyone could answer, one of the old vampires sneezed himself off of his chair. When a Nurse picked him up, he was oozing boogers.

"I'm. So. Tired!" he wailed, and passed out.

"We'd better just hurry," said Shane, helping Griselda.

"Yes, the residents are getting delirious," said a very concerned Director Z. "I really want to administer this treatment as quickly as possible."

"Let's make sure everyone gets the same amount," said Nabila, and she grabbed one of the soup ladles on the table.

"Yeah, and make sure we get some," said Gordon. "I'm already feeling sick again."

"We can always ask the ghosts to make more," I said. "Although I'd rather not, if we don't have to."

The old monsters stared at us strangely through their weak watery eyes as we scooped out sloppy, goopy snot with booger chunks.

"What is that?" Clarice the banshee asked.

"Pietro said this was ghost snot," replied Frederick.

"I don't believe a thing Pietro says," said Clarice, and she ate a spoonful. "Ugh, this is terrible!"

"So it is ghost snot?" asked Queen Hatshepsut, the oldest of the mummies in residence. "Oh, I can't do it."

She pushed her plate back.

"You have to eat it," said Shane. "You guys are going to feel better."

The old zombies had a stronger reaction to the boogers than the other old monsters did.

"Garrrrrr!" yelled one, and threw his booger bowl at Director Z's face.

"People, people!" yelled Director Z, green chunks dripping down his face. "Please, remain calm. I know that everyone is exhausted, but Ben assures me that eating this will help you. Just ask Pietro."

"Oh, this stuff is disgusting!" yelled Pietro. "It wasn't this bad the first time."

"Maybe because it's so fresh?" I wondered out loud.

The old monsters that could were starting to stand up and walk away from the tables. A Nurse shoved a spoonful into Griselda's mouth, and she immediately hacked it up.

Director Z caught a booger that crept down his face with his tongue and almost gagged when he started chewing.

"Oh my," he said. "This actually is pretty bad."

Shane sucked down a spoonful and almost immediately barfed up the green goodies.

"Terrible," he shrieked.

More monsters were throwing booger bowls.

"Wait, wait!" I said, scooping up handfuls of snot

off the raggedy old carpet. "Stop doing that! We'll figure something out. Don't waste it! It's magical, I swear."

"Vell, it's not magical if ve can't eat it," snorted Grigore.

"Well, VHAT do you VANT me to do, cook you a booger pie?" I asked, frustrated.

"Hey," said Shane. "That doesn't sound like a bad idea."

"Booger sauce over pasta?" asked Ben.

"Booger pâté?" offered Nabila, and then, "No, no, it's too hard to cook."

"Fresh garden salad with booger bits?" Shane tried.

"Booger casserole with chicken and noodles?" I asked. "Wait, even better—Mac 'n' Sneeze!"

"Real-life Mac 'n' Sneeze," chuckled Gordon, then the visual of it hit him. "Oh, I think I'm going to hurl."

We looked at Director Z.

"All right," he said. "Let's have a dinner party! The Nurses and I will try to calm down the residents as much as we can."

He wiped off his face with a handkerchief and handed it to me.

"Here," he said. "For your booger pie."

Hungry for Boogers

Once we had gathered as much of the snot as we could, we instructed the chefs in the kitchen on how to perfect our creations.

"The boogers should be super crispy," said Shane to one chef. "Nice and crunchy, so it really complements the bacon in the salad. Fry them hard, and don't be afraid of oversalting."

"Hmmmm," said Gordon, peering under the arm of another towering chef, as he mixed furiously. "Maybe we should throw the cheese sauce in a blender before adding the macaroni. It's a little chunky right now."

I was about to tell my chef to add more eggs to my

booger pie, when Director Z came into the room.

"Chris, can I have a word with you?" he asked, adding, "in private?"

"Sure," I said. "You guys need to figure out a main course. Maybe roast chicken with herbs and boogers?"

"So, not 'original recipe'?" Shane giggled.

"I think the walk-in refrigerator will be the perfect place to speak," said Director Z, and opened the door for me.

I'd been having a great time in the kitchen and had almost forgotten about our situation. As the door shut, I began to get worried.

"What's going on?" I asked.

"Chris, I fear that the puppies and kittens are more powerful than we think," he said. "Or they're just a precursor of something worse."

"What do you mean?" I asked. "Once the monsters eat dinner, we'll be good to go!"

"Maybe," said Director Z. "Or maybe not. I'm still trying to figure out how the puppies and kittens got here in the first place, and I fear that it may be the work of someone on the inside."

"You mean a traitor?" I gasped. "One of the old monsters is a traitor?"

"I just don't know," said Director Z. "In addition, the team sent to investigate and deal with the puppies and kittens is no longer communicating with me. I fear they may have been destroyed. I have a very bad feeling about this."

"What do you need from me?" I asked.

"I need you to carry something for me," he said, loosening his tie.

"Your pendant?" I asked.

"Indeed," he said, and pulled a chain out from under his shirt. A piece of bloodstone hung from the bottom.

"I had two of these in my possession—mine and one that had belonged to my old mentor," he said. "And now the other one is gone. I thought I had hidden it well enough in this old manor, but apparently I was wrong. Someone has gotten to it. If this is all the work of a traitor, they'll most likely be after this one as well."

He handed his pendant over to me. It was strangely heavy.

"I cannot stress enough how important this task is that I'm about to give you," he said. "Humans have only just recently begun wielding pendants. It used to be only senior monsters that held them—those that were tasked with saving their kind. The second pendant—the one that I spoke of before, the one that was stolen—was the last to be worn by a senior monster Keeper. He was a wonderful Cyclops by the name of Percy. I had been meaning to find a Keeper to replace him, but quite frankly, we've lost so many residents that there was no need for a new facility. Percy's pendant would have been much safer off this property . . ."

Director Z looked off into the back of the cold, refrigerated room, lost in thought.

"Director Z?" I asked. "Should I hide this one? Maybe I could give it to the ghosts?"

"No," he said, snapping back to attention. "No, you must hold it. At this point, I don't trust anyone, especially that old cutlass-wielding ghost who has it in for my residents. I don't trust anyone but you, Chris."

I started to put the necklace around my neck.

"Wait," said Director Z. "Keep it on you, but don't wear it. It would be too easily seen."

"Okay," I said, and I put the pendant in my pocket.

"You are a Keeper now, Chris," said Director Z. "If anything happens to me—"

"What's going to happen to you?" I said, afraid.

"*If* anything happens to me," he continued, "you'll be in charge. The Nurses will follow your every order. The residents will have no choice but to fall in line under the power of the pendant."

He pulled another pendant out of his suit coat pocket.

"Wait, I thought you said you lost the other one," I said.

"Oh, I did," he said. "This one is a fake. If someone comes looking for the other pendant—my pendant—I want them to think I still have it. And you have to play along with me. No matter what happens—"

"What's going to *happen*!?" I said, really upset now.

"No matter what happens," continued Director Z, "you must play along that this is the real pendant. Understood?"

"Understood," I confirmed.

Within an hour, the family-style booger feast was ready. We helped the chefs carry out our crazy creations.

"It looks so good, I just drooled a little," said Gordon. "I don't even feel like hurling. Do I like eating boogers now? Have I become that guy, the booger eater?"

"This is going to be amazing," said Ben. "Amazing."

"I dunno," I said. "They might not even be hungry for real food—they all look terrible. Three more have passed out. We're going to have to hand-feed some of them."

A few of the old monsters reached out and grabbed spoonfuls of food and put it on their plates. The sounds of sneezes and snotting still filled the air, and a few of the older monsters that hadn't already passed out kept falling out of their chairs. Nurses held a few in place and not-so-gently shoved spoonfuls of food into their mouths.

"I wish we had made a big soup," Shane said. "Split-pea. The boogers would have blended right in and the weaker monsters wouldn't be having such a hard time."

We gathered around a large plate of food to share. We didn't want to eat too much—the monsters needed it the most.

"Man, I'm pretty proud of us," I said. "I don't think anyone would think all of this was made with ghost boogers."

"I feel great, too," Nabila said. "In fact . . . "

She sniffed a long, hard sniff.

"I think I can smell!" she said. "Barely . . . but I can smell!!"

"No way!" we all yelled.

"This is amazing," she said, and hugged Ben. "What's that smell?"

"Um . . . ," Ben looked down nervously.

"That's what is known to those who can smell as 'stinky armpits,'" said Gordon through a mouthful of salad.

"That's what those smell like . . . ," she said, a sour look on her face.

"Sorry," said Ben. "But, since you couldn't smell, I didn't spend much time scrubbing in the shower. And I sort of ran out of deodorant."

"Just wait until you smell his barf," I said, chuckling.

The noise level rose in the dining room as the old

monsters slowly came back to life.

"I vant more!" yelled Grigore, and he plunged his spoon back into the Mac 'n' Sneeze.

"Grrrrrrr," growled Pietro and Howie as they fought over a chicken leg.

"Look," said Ben. "Even the older ones are starting to get into it."

Instead of holding up weak old monsters, the Nurses were struggling to get food on plates fast enough.

Old Bigfoot was chowing down on my booger pie, and with each bite, his fur glistened a little more. He stood up straighter.

"It's working," said Ben. "It's really working. Roy's back!"

"Ow!" shrieked Grigore. "There's something under my dentures. Vhat did you put into this?"

I rushed over to Grigore with Shane.

"Just take them out," said Shane. "I'll take a look."

Grigore pulled out his dentures.

"No way!" yelled Shane. "There are teeth under your dentures."

"Vhat?" Grigore gasped and put a finger into his mouth. "Ouch! They're sharp. I love it!"

"Look," I said to Shane. "He's getting his hair back."

Grigore reached up to his head, which was sprouting fuzzy black hair.

"Stop bothering me—I've gotta eat!" he cried with joy.

Up and down the table, the monsters were getting younger by the second.

"This is amazing," said Director Z. "Gentlemen, you've done it again! The residents look healthier than they have in years!"

"Mmmmm," shrieked Murrayhotep, and he jumped up onto the table. "This tastes amazing! OM NOM NOM!"

He shoved handfuls of whatever he could grab into his mouth.

"Hey!" shrieked Clarice as Murrayhotep snatched a meatball and strands of pasta from her plate. "What are you *doing*?!"

"Murray, stop that this instant!" yelled Director Z.

But Murrayhotep kept going, on his hands and knees, down the long table, eating and screaming and flinging food everywhere.

"What's gotten into him?" wondered Shane. "He was the only one that wasn't sick."

"Murray, this is my last warning," said Director Z.

In response, Murray grabbed the roast chicken in the middle of the table and flung it as hard as he could at Director Z, knocking him back.

"NURSES!" yelled Director Z from the floor, and the Nurses moved in to detain Murrayhotep.

"You just try and get me, you brainless oafs!" he yelled.

"Get back," yelled Pietro, and not-so-old monsters jumped back from their chairs and away from the table.

A Nurse grabbed Murrayhotep by his leg, and he came crashing facedown on the table.

He quickly turned right-side up and smashed his foot into the jaw of the Nurse, who went down hard onto the floor.

"Ha-ha-haaa!" yelled Murrayhotep. "Serves you right."

"Where is he getting the energy?" asked Gordon.

"He just ate half of the food," I said.

Two Nurses moved in on either side of the table and reached up to grab Murrayhotep.

"*INUM-RA!*" yelled Murrayhotep as he flung his hands outward. There was a flash, and the Nurses were flung to either wall.

Director Z, who was wiping boogery chicken off of his suit, stood up and faced Murrayhotep.

"This is preposterous!" yelled Director Z, so loudly that the dining room windows rattled.

"This *is* preposterous!" Murrayhotep yelled back. "Our kind is nearing the brink of extinction, and *humans* have been put in charge of our safekeeping? I've had enough!"

Murrayhotep raised the palms of his bandaged

hands toward Director Z. Everyone stood in shock.

"*OSIRIS-MUN-RA!*"

Thousands of scarab beetles buzzed out of Murrayhotep's palms, descending upon Director Z, who fell to the floor, screaming.

"Feast, my precious ones!" yelled Murrayhotep. "Feast until you taste bone!"

Your Mummy
Doesn't Love You

"*KHEPRI-RA-ATUM*," yelled Nabila, her hands held high.

A great wind blew through the dining room. The chitter-chattering scarabs were blown off of Director Z and back onto Murrayhotep.

He dropped onto the table, flailing wildly, trying to fight off the beetles.

"Where did you learn to do that?" Ben asked.

"I'll tell you later," Nabila replied, running to Director Z, whose face was pockmarked with tiny bites.

As we helped the Director up, he turned to Nabila.

"Thank you," he said.

"That was AWESOME," yelled Shane.

"*RA-MUN-OSIRIS!*" yelled Murrayhotep, and the scarabs flew off his body and exploded, a thousand small pops. He ran off of the table in a flash.

"Get him!" I yelled.

The entire room got up and rushed to the door—not-so-old monsters, kids, and all. Murrayhotep stopped in front of the doorway, his tattered wrappings flapping slightly, his breathing heavy.

"I will not run from you," said the old mummy with a wild look in his eyes. "It is *you* who shall run from *me*."

We all stood facing him, a large angry wall of monsters and kids, ready.

"You sure about that?" asked Shane. The monsters behind him growled and bared their teeth.

Murrayhotep raised his hand and displayed his huge gold ring for a moment, before grabbing the black gemstone in its center and turning it with a click.

"What are you doing?" I asked.

"Something I should have done long ago," said Murrayhotep. "Taking control of my afterlife. Doing something worthwhile."

"What are you getting out of this?" I screamed. "Eternal life? And you would throw away all of your friends here?"

"I was promised that I would be reunited with my sister," he said. "And I would do anything for her. You would have been destroyed in good time, anyway."

Lt. Commander Stratford entered the room, his gnarled, ghostly hand gripping his short sword tighter than ever.

"ALARM! The beastly animals are on their way down the hallway to you," he yelled, swinging his sword around.

"What?" gasped a few not-so-old monsters.

"Why would you care?" I asked the old ghost. "You've had it out for the monsters since they got here."

"Now that I know *who* brought them here," said the Lt. Commander, "I can focus my energies on him. I took the liberty of floating into his room and peeking at his papyrus diary. Luckily, I can decipher hieroglyphs—thanks to my time with the British Expeditionary Force in Egypt. I'm talking about you, you whippersnapper!"

He raised his short sword at Murrayhotep's head.

"You brought the animals?" asked Director Z.

"It's true," Murrayhotep said, and hundreds of puppies and kittens filed behind him as he raised his golden ring again.

"Then you have betrayed us." Director Z spoke gravely.

Murrayhotep turned the ring once more.

"EEEEEEEEEEEEEE!" The animals screamed and thrashed on the floor.

"What's wrong with them?" screeched Nabila as she covered her ears.

The werewolves howled along in agony with the tiny animals. The banshees screeched.

"Ha-ha-ha-haaaaaa!" yelled Murrayhotep. "Be free, little ones, be free!"

And with a great SPLUNK, black, leathery wings burst out of the backs of the puppies and kittens. The screaming turned to screechy laughing as the animals' heads stretched out, fur exploding into long, lizard-like faces with sharp, sharp fangs. Their jaws stretched and their teeth clamped together as they transformed.

"I knew those little guys had something in them," screeched Lt. Commander Stratford, and he floated out of the room. "I'm going to get help!"

"What are those things?" Ben asked.

"Meet the sangala!" hissed Murrayhotep. "The bringers of your doom!"

The leathery lizard animals took flight, their wings WHAPWHAPWHAPing, and hovered behind Murrayhotep. Some of them began drooling a hot, sticky drool that sizzled and hissed as it hit the floor.

We stood face-to-face with the newest monster juice–drinking enemy. The monsters lined up behind us hissed and swatted at the air.

"Attack Formation Delta Four!" screamed Shane.

The vampires all turned into bats and floated high up to the wooden beams of the dining room.

"Wow, they got so big," marveled Gordon. "Those

boogers really worked some magic."

"Did they work enough magic, though?" Ben wondered.

Moth Man soon followed the bats into the eaves. The werewolves turned into wolf form and padded out in front of us, teeth exposed. The tallest monsters, Frederick and Roy, headed to the front. The rest did their best to make sure the oldest monsters were mixed in with the strongest.

"It's going to be hard to deal with the fact that these nasty things can fly," said Gordon as we formed a circle. He turned to Shane. "I'm glad you insisted on the buddy system for the older, weaker ones."

The witches threw up a protective charm in front of us and then rushed to the kitchen to prepare for the wounded. Half of the Nurses stood near the kitchen, to help wounded monsters into the makeshift infirmary. The others headed up front with the tallest monsters.

The Director stood next to us and raised the same metal cylinder he had given us to clean out the drains. He powered it up, and a bolt of electricity flashed out of the front like a whip. He swung the electro-whip over his head.

"Whoa," said Shane, wide-eyed. "He didn't tell us it could do that!"

"It's your move, old man," said Director Z.

"Destroy them," Murrayhotep commanded the

animals, "but leave the Director unharmed. He is mine!"

The sangala swarmed.

Director Z, with a crack of his electro-whip, began knocking down sangala one by one. Nurses rushed up to crush the flopping creatures on the floor with their massive boots. Werewolves stood at the ready to tear apart the ones the Nurses missed.

One werewolf jumped off of the dining room table and snatched a sangala in its mouth as it came tumbling down to the ground.

CHOMP.

Murrayhotep ran up to Director Z, knocking him down onto the ground.

"Ooof!" yelled Director Z as he hit his butt hard. His electro-whip turned off as it fell from his hand and rattled into the crowd of clashing monsters and sangala.

Director Z's fake pendant came up around his neck and dangled in front of his tie.

"YESSSSSS!" screeched Murrayhotep, and he lunged for Director Z and his prize.

"Not so fast, Hotep," yelled Gordon, tackling Murrayhotep.

He wrestled Murrayhotep to the ground, pinning him in place.

"Arrrgh!" yelled Murrayhotep, who struggled, then pinned Gordon. They were stuck together—a crazy, sweaty pretzel.

Director Z headed into the battle with the monsters and sangala, searching for his weapon.

"My children," Murrayhotep croaked from under Gordon, "come and help me."

A dozen sangala, who were battling the vampire bats up above, swooped down toward the struggling Gordon and Murrayhotep.

"Karate shield!" yelled Shane.

Shane, Ben, Nabila, and I stood around Gordon and Murrayhotep and began karate-chopping down sangala as they floated in. They snapped and snarled, flapping their wings like crazy.

SCREEESCREEESCREEE!

Our hands hit their faces with leathery THUMPS.

"Aaaahhh!" yelled Shane, and he clutched his right hand. "Watch their fangs!"

"Your hand is smoking!" screeched Nabila, knocking back another sangala.

"It hurts!" cried Shane. "We need help over here! Zombies!"

From the crowd, which was beginning to fill with the screams of now-old monsters, Director Z pushed a few zombies toward us.

"Scream if you need more," he said, and then raised his electro-whip in time to avoid being dive-bombed by a sangala.

They karate-chopped their way toward us.

On the floor, Gordon and Murrayhotep continued to struggle.

"Let me loose now," hissed Murrayhotep, "and I promise to leave you children unscathed."

"Yeah, right!" said Gordon, and he twisted Murrayhotep's arm.

"Waaaaaargh!" Murrayhotep cried. "You'll pay for that!"

The zombies joined us, surrounding Murrayhotep and Gordon. They weren't very accurate, but they made for a good shield, constantly chopping at whatever was in front of them.

They were followed by a severed arm, walking on two tiny claws, the hand swaying back and forth.

It skittered past us and out the door.

"What was that?" asked Ben.

"Pay attention to the sangala," I said, ducking just in time to save my nose from a juicy, fangy SNAP.

"Aaaaaah," an old monster screamed.

Then a huge hairy leg, also walking upright on two tiny claws, skittered past.

"What was *that*?" asked Shane, pointing into the crowd. "Ugh, is that going to happen to me?"

I looked into the crowd to see Bigfoot with one less big foot.

I looked at Shane's hand, which was raw, bruised, and still smoking.

"Stick it in the booger pie," I said.

Shane ran over to the table, and we kept swatting off the sangala. One of the zombies missed his target, and a sangala bit into his arm, zombie blood and sangala drool flying everywhere.

His arm turned green and tore itself from his body, landing on the floor. It sprouted two small claws, jumped up, and ran off.

"My arrrrrrm!" the zombie moaned.

"You have another arm," I yelled. "Don't just stand there!"

The sangala attack intensified, and arms and legs swarmed past us and out the door in droves.

"I can't hold on much longer," grunted Gordon.

"Get OFF!" yelled Murrayhotep.

"The booger pie worked," Shane screamed. "Everyone, eat the leftovers for a power boost."

A few legless monsters hopped over to the table and began to chow down.

Almost immediately, new legs grew back into place with a POP.

"Wow, that's amazing," yelled Ben.

A few sangala swooped past the stunned Ben to bite Gordon and help their master.

"Wah," Gordon yelled, and flipped Murrayhotep on top of his body, shielding himself from the sangala, which could not hurt their master.

Murrayhotep jumped up, triumphant, and headed toward the main battle.

"ANUBIS-MAR-DUN," screamed Nabila.

Murrayhotep stopped in his tracks and turned around to face Nabila.

"How DARE you," he hissed.

"What did you do?" I asked.

Before she could answer, Murrayhotep's wrappings started unwrapping themselves.

"Arrrrrggh!" screamed Murrayhotep.

The wrappings flew up into the air and rained down on us. The sangala flew away, dodging the wrappings.

SHRRRRRRRPPPPP!

They seemed to go on forever, until the ends finally floated down on us.

Murrayhotep stood before us, completely naked.

He ran out of the room, his frazzled, dried mummy butt shaking slightly as he flew down the hallway.

"A mummy with no wrappings has no power," said Nabila.

We cheered, still covered in the wrappings.

"Amazing," said Shane, and high-fived her. "Ow . . . my hand still hurts."

"More booger pie?" I asked.

Shane looked over at the table.

"It's all gone," he said.

A half dozen more arms and legs ran past us and out of the door.

"Help, gentlemen, help!" screamed Director Z.

He was the only one left standing in the room aside from us, swatting at the two dozen sangala that flew just above his head, trying desperately to keep them at bay.

Old monsters writhed on the floor, and arms and legs were popping off everywhere. From the kitchen, more screams could be heard—the wounded and dying.

"Oh no!" yelled Nabila.

The sangala swooped down on the monsters.

Let's Wrap
It Up

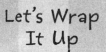

"CHAAAAAAARGE!" yelled a voice, and Lt. Commander Stratford appeared with his family, Leila and all, to swoop down on the sangala.

"SNOOOOOOOOTTTTT!" he yelled again, and each of the ghosts floated to a sangala . . .

SNIFFFFFFFFFF!

. . . and sneezed.

SNOOOOOOOOORRRRFFFFBLLLLL!

Delicious glowing green boogers rained down on the monsters.

"Eat!" yelled Richard. "Eat, my friends."

But the monsters couldn't eat. They were overwhelmed by the sangala, who continued their furious attack. Director Z couldn't lash them back fast enough, and the ghosts couldn't do anything but snot more.

"I have an idea!" yelled Nabila. "The wrappings! The sangala left us alone once they landed all over us. Maybe they still think the wrappings are their master."

"Wrap yourself in one," I yelled, and wrapped myself in one long piece of cloth. "Ew, I can smell Murrayhotep's BO."

The others quickly did the same, bundling up in Murrayhotep's stinky old wrappings.

"WAAAAAAAAH!" We ran at the battleground in the dining room, screaming our heads off to scare the sangala.

The sangala kept chewing on the monsters until we ran into the crowd. They floated up, confused to see five Murrayhoteps. The ghosts floated through the sangala and sneezed once more, another booger shower.

"Sneeze on the monsters in the kitchen, too," I yelled at the ghosts.

"Snot on us! Snot on us!" they chanted from the kitchen.

The monsters on the floor ate and licked and guzzled boogers and snot, fighting for their lives. Arms and legs popped back into place. The vampire bats circled above us.

"Grigore," I yelled, and one of the bats, now a little

grayer, flew down to me. "Let me wrap this around you."

I ripped off some of my wrappings and wrapped them around Bat Grigore.

"Let's use the wrappings to lead all of the sangala into the walk-in refrigerator," I said. "It's a much smaller space, and we can finish them off there!"

The monsters all rose, stunned, old, and busted—but with all of their legs and arms in place.

"Grigore!" I yelled. "Keep them from flying up too high!"

We slowly stumbled forward, pushing the sangala toward the kitchen. Bat Grigore did a great job of keeping them lower, and we got them through the door.

A werewolf, newly revived from the boogers that the ghosts had rained down in the kitchen, lunged up to grab a low-flying sangala, and a few broke off and back into the dining room.

"Wait, wait!" I yelled at the werewolf. "We have to wait until they get into the walk-in refrigerator."

"I'll handle the few that went back into the dining room!" yelled Director Z. "Nurse Inx, Nurse Grob—come with me."

They headed back into the dining room as we pushed deeper into the kitchen. Monsters noshed on boogers in preparation for the final battle in the walk-in refrigerator.

The sangala spat and snarled and snapped at us and

Bat Grigore, but had no choice. They couldn't harm us, and we wouldn't let them get past us.

"Just a little farther!" I yelled. "Steady!"

We pushed them all into the walk-in refrigerator, and they smashed into jars and snarled at boxes of food as they looked for a way out.

But there was no way out.

"All right," I yelled. "Get 'em, guys!"

We stepped out of the doorway, and dozens of zombies, werewolves, vampires, and more spilled into the room, crushing, crunching, and grabbing.

SCREEEEEEEEEEP!

The sangala's screeches were cut off as the last one was crushed between the jaws of Pietro.

"Yeah!" we all yelled, jumping around with relief.

We peeked back into the walk-in refrigerator.

"Ew," said Ben.

"Gnarly," said Gordon.

The room was covered in the green guts and leathery parts of the sangala.

The monsters all roared with happiness.

And then there was a great BOOOOOM from the dining room.

Escape from Gallow Manor

We rushed into the dining room to find two Nurses lying on the floor, and a newly wrapped Murrayhotep leaning over a disarmed Director Z.

"Is that toilet paper?" asked Shane. "I hope it's double-ply, or it won't last for long."

"The pendants shall be mine!" yelled Murrayhotep, and he grabbed for the chain on Director Z's neck.

BLURRZZZZZT!

Murrayhotep was thrown off of Director Z.

Director Z stood up boldly, strolling toward Murrayhotep.

"Did you really think I hadn't put a protective charm on it?" yelled Director Z.

Murrayhotep slowly stood up, his toilet paper wrappings drooping a bit.

"Well, then," Murrayhotep snarled, "I guess I'll have to kill you."

"If I die, the pendant loses its power," Director Z said.

The still-drained-but-at-least-they-had-all-their-limbs monsters came into the room. They snarled and clawed the air, upset to see Murrayhotep again.

"I don't have time for this!" Murrayhotep screeched. "I'm taking you to him! He'll know what to do!"

Murrayhotep raised his arms: "*AMON-RA-NAMAN!*"

Director Z collapsed like a sack of potatoes.

"Noooo!" I screeched, and ran toward Director Z. I threw myself down on the floor and grabbed his face.

"The moon's face is the perfect place for record keeping," said Director Z, and then he passed out completely.

"Get back, you dog!" Murrayhotep yelled, kicking me with his toilet-papered foot.

I slid all the way to the wall, clutching my belly. I felt like I was going to throw up—blood.

"Are you okay?" asked Shane.

"Let's just *get* him," I gasped.

But Murrayhotep had a head start. He had already

thrown Director Z over his shoulder and was running down the hall.

Shane yanked me up to my feet, and we thundered down the hall with our friends and the older-again monsters.

Murrayhotep ran into the North Wing, opened the small iron door on the wall, and sent the gate crashing down. We slammed against the gate, monsters pushing us up against the bars.

"Everyone stop pushing!" I grunted. "You're gonna crush us."

"He can't take the Director," screeched a banshee.

Old Bigfoot pushed his way through the crowd and grabbed the bottom of the gate.

"RAAAAAWWWWRRR!" he grunted, and the gate slowly rose.

There was about a foot of room from the floor to the bottom of the gate.

"Goooooooo!" he said. "Can't. Hold. For. Long."

Ben, Shane, Gordon, Nabila, and I slid through, and the gate came crashing down again.

"Shane and Nabila," I yelled. "We have to catch up with him. Ben and Gordon, open the gate for the others."

The three of us rushed down to the end of the hall, where a mysterious open door led to the grounds.

"Hey, where did this door come from?" Shane asked as we burst through and could see Murrayhotep in the moonlight up ahead, running for the forest.

"It's too far for me to throw a spell on him," Nablia said, gasping.

"Hurry," I huffed.

We had almost caught up to Murrayhotep when he hit the forest.

"I can't see anything," I said as we entered the thick, tall trees.

"Over there!" yelled Shane.

"Is he bringing him to a tree trunk?" I said. "That tree is huge."

"It's not a tree," said Nabila. "It's a spaceship. A huge rocket."

"No way!" I gasped.

Murrayhotep ran up to the tall, oil-black, shiny ship, and placed his hand on the door. A light shone into the forest as the door slowly hummed open. Inside the opening, monster arms and legs walked around.

"So that's where they were running to," said Shane.

Murrayhotep rushed inside, and the door began to close.

"Go!" I yelled. "We can make it!"

We rushed up to the door, just as it slid back into place.

We slammed into the cold hard metal.

"Noooooo!" I yelled, kicking the ship.

A great vibration shook our feet.

"No time for anger," Shane said. "This thing's gonna take off!"

We ran back toward the grounds of the manor. At the forest's edge, monsters started to zoom past us.

"Guys, no!" I yelled. "Get back to the manor!"

The monsters, who normally never listened to me, turned back and ran with us.

There was a great roar, and a bright light, as the ship took off, blowing us all over the grounds in a burst of hot wind. I rolled until I hit the bush shaped like a raven and watched the ship take off into the night.

The Moon's Face

We rushed to the West Tower of the manor, and I swung up my telescope.

"Where is he going?" asked Nabila.

I focused on the ship and then pulled back a little. The ship was tall, with strange spines jutting out of the sides, and a green glow propelled it through the atmosphere. It was so black, I shouldn't have seen it, but its surface shone like crazy.

"The moon," I gasped. "It's headed right for the moon."

"No way!" said Ben.

"The moon . . . ," I said, trying hard to think.

"What?" asked Shane.

"Before he passed out, Director Z said, 'The moon's face is the perfect place for record keeping.'"

"What does that mean?" asked Gordon.

"I have no idea . . . ," I said, staring again through the telescope at the moon's face.

The moon winked at me.

"Huh?" I said, shocked, pulling my face back. "It's like the moon has a real face . . . just like . . ."

"What!?" Nabila screeched, dying of anticipation.

"Just like the face of the moon in that weird room I saw." I gasped. "Guys, follow me!"

We rushed downstairs to the dining room.

The stronger monsters were helping the Nurses clean the dining room, though most of the monsters had gone to bed to get some rest.

"It was this door," I said, stopping in front of the weird room. "This is where I saw it!"

I turned the handle . . . and the door opened.

We rushed in, and I pointed up to the grainy old photo.

"See?" I asked.

"Totally cool," said Shane.

Gordon closed the door, and we found ourselves in a small library, with a model of the solar system hanging from the ceiling. The planets were all metal balls. I opened a closet to find a metallic space suit with a glass helmet.

"I just need to figure out what kind of records we're looking for," I said, biting my bottom lip.

"Well, there are plenty of books here," said Ben, pulling one out of a bookshelf with a puff of dust. "This one's on the effects of zero gravity."

"This one's about the great wars of the Andromeda Galaxy," said Nabila, opening another.

"What's this?" asked Gordon, holding up a small black cylinder.

"I think that's an old record," said Shane. "I saw one once in a museum."

"A record!" I said. "'The perfect place for record keeping.' Director Z must want us to listen to that record."

"Didn't we see an old phonograph in one of the rooms?" asked Shane.

"Yeah!" replied Nabila. "But which one . . ."

"The music room?" Gordon said.

"No," said Ben. "The bear-rug room?"

"No," I said, frustrated. "This place is too big! It doesn't matter. We all remember seeing one. Let's go find it."

We found it in the game room, tucked behind the chessboard in the corner.

"How do we work it?" I asked. "Any guesses?"

"Well," said Shane, grabbing the cylinder. "It looks like the cylinder fits here."

He clicked it into place.

"I think you crank this handle," said Gordon, and started to crank.

"Put the needle on the record," said Nabila.

"It looks like it's going to scratch it like crazy," I said.

"Just do it!" said Ben.

I put the needle down on the cylinder, and a great scratching sound came out of the huge cone at the top of the phonograph.

SCHHLLLRRPPHHHSCHHLLLRRPPHHH!

"I think we broke it!" I said.

Then, out of the scratching, came a voice.

"Journal entry dated July 24, 1892. Today, my work is finally finished. The Stratford family has been kind enough to endure all of my late-night madness and the strange clanking from deep below their dungeon. I will have to thank them for the use of their manor for years to come. But it is finally complete. A fully functional spaceship, capable of transporting over one hundred souls, set on a course to the moon. Unfortunately, I have lost my previous creation, Frederick, a monster crafted of human flesh and brought to life by electricity. He escaped from his home weeks ago, and I would have hoped to have found him by now. For only he can sit in the captain's chair and power the great ship into the cosmos with his strange electrical energies."

"Did Frederick make it through the sangala attack?" I asked.

"I think so," said Ben.

"Well, it sounds like all we need to do is get him into the captain's chair of that ship that's hiding somewhere deep below the dungeon," I said, "and we can save Director Z."

"On the MOON?" asked Nabila. "I can't go to the moon! I have to ask my parents' permission first."

"I'd like to see *that* conversation," Ben said, snickering.

"I don't think this is the kind of thing you ask permission for . . . ," I said.

"This is crazy," said Gordon. "We're going to the moon."

"To the MOON!" yelled Shane.

"My dream come true!" I yelled, suddenly insanely excited.

"Was your dream to go to the moon with a ship full of monsters?" asked Nabila. "Because we're going to need them for whatever's up there. We can't do it alone."

"Ah, so you're ready to go now?" asked Gordon.

"Monsters in space," said Shane. "I think I saw that movie when I was a little kid."

"Oh no!" I said, slapping my forehead.

"What is it?" asked Nabila.

"The moon," I said. "Because of the lunar cycle and the time of day, I think . . ."

"What?" Shane asked, pulling my hand off my forehead.

"Oh, man . . ." I didn't want to tell them until I was sure.

I pushed away from Shane and rushed to the bookshelves, pulling out books like a madman. "This isn't what I'm looking for," I screeched, tossing dusty old books to the floor.

"What is it?" yelled Ben, upset that I was so upset.

I ran over to a large table, which was piled high with charts and diagrams. I frantically dug through the pile, finally finding what I was looking for: a dusty, yellowed old launch-window chart.

"Yes!" I yelled, and held it up for closer study. "NO!"

"WHAT IS IT!?!" yelled all four of my friends.

"The current window for launch to the moon is going to close in"—I looked at my iPhone—"forty-five minutes."

"Okay, so we'll wait a few days," said Nabila. "I need to think up a story to tell my parents, anyway."

"No," I said, studying the crusty document. "It could be more than a few days—even a week or two before the next window opens. Who knows what they'll do to Director Z before then. We have to go NOW!"

"All right," said Shane. "Let's find Frederick. Then

we've got to find the ship. And then we'll blast out of here!"

"All right, all right," said Ben and Gordon.

"Fine," said Nabila. "But we're all going to be in huge trouble."

"Not as much trouble as Director Z is in," I said. "We've got to move fast."

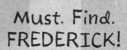

Must. Find.
FREDERICK!

"The East Wing is clear," said Gordon. "No sign of Frederick?"

Monsters shuffled into the foyer from different parts of the manor.

"Nothing," said Clarice.

"Where did he go?" asked Medusa. Her snakes hissed sadly.

"FREDERICK!!!" Roy's voice boomed through the foyer. All of us—monsters, boys, and girl—waited for a sound.

NOTHING.

"Now that I think of it," said Pietro, "I don't seem to remember seeing him after the battle. Maybe his head came off and ran into the spaceship."

"Ew," I said.

Nabila shuddered.

"No, no, no," said Shane. "I'm sure that I saw him."

"Pietro," I said to the old werewolf. "We've only got twenty minutes left. Come with the five of us to Frederick's room, and give it a good sniff."

"I'm no bloodhound," said Pietro.

"You are today," said Gordon, who slapped Pietro on the back. "Maybe your nose can tell us something."

Pietro turned into a wolf and padded down the West Wing into Frederick's room. We followed.

Sniff, sniff, sniiiiiiiff!

Pietro sniffed around the old stitched-together monster's room. Then he pushed his snout out of the room and sniffed the hallway.

"Anything?" asked Ben.

"Grrrr . . . ," grumbled Pietro, shaking his mangy head *no*.

"Wait," I said, walking over to the laundry basket in the room. "I think this will help."

I opened it up, and used the tips of my fingers to grab a dirty pair of Frederick's tighty-whities.

"Ick," I yelled, tossing them at Pietro.

Sniff, sniff . . . HOOOOOOWWWWL!

Pietro was off, racing down the hallway, back toward the foyer.

"Hurry!" I yelled, running after him. My friends followed.

In the foyer, he took a sharp left toward the North Wing, and then with a great SCREEEECH of nails, changed his mind and decided to go down the East Wing instead.

"Don't you DARE lick my face again," Lucinda B. Smythe screeched as Pietro ran past.

We burst through the huge doors and followed Pietro to the organ keyboard at the back of the banquet hall.

Pietro stopped in front of the keyboard, barking furiously.

"What's next?" Ben knelt down and asked the werewolf. Drool sprayed into his face. "Is he behind the keyboard? Can't you change back to human form and tell us what's happening?"

"WAIT!" I said. "He might be naked. You never know—sometimes they lose their clothes when they change."

"Don't!" yelled Gordon.

I held my hands over my eyes, but Pietro just kept barking. Then he lifted a paw up onto the organ, and three sour notes echoed through the huge, empty room.

"You want us to play it?" I asked.

"Look!" said Nabila, pointing at a key. "This one's more worn than the others. And this one. That one, too."

She pushed the frothing werewolf to the side, and pushed down on all three keys at once.

With a great creak, the organ keyboard jerked forward, throwing Nabila on her rump. Then, with a great scrape of wood and stone, it slid to the left.

"A secret stairway!" Nabila said. "I knew it!"

With another bark, Pietro jumped down spiraling stairs.

"Are you sure we should—?" Ben tried to ask, but the rest of us followed Pietro.

"Okay, okay, I'm coming," huffed Ben.

"This reminds me of going down into the vampire crypt at Raven Hill," said Shane. "Ah, the good old days."

"Don't talk," said Gordon. "I'm getting dizzy."

Candles on the wall gave us a little light, but there was something brighter at the bottom.

We made our way to a locked iron door with torches at either side. Pietro started barking like crazy again. We jiggled at the handle, and pushed the door, but . . .

"Nothing!" I grunted. "Ugh! We've got ten minutes left! How are we going to get behind that door, find Frederick, and then find the ship?"

"I can help," Quincy said from stairs. "Let me see what's on the other side."

"Oh, Quincy!" yelled Nabila. "That's a great idea. How did you know we were down here?"

"I've been following you this whole time!" he said.

"This is the most fun I've ever had in the manor."

"If Frederick is on the other side, tell him to open the door," Nabila said.

"I will!" said Quincy, and he floated through the door.

Pietro finally stopped barking, and it was silent at the bottom of the stairs.

After what felt like an eternity, Quincy popped his head through the door with a "Boo!"

"Wah!" yelled Nabila. "Stop doing that to me! What's the news!?"

"Frederick is on the other side," said Quincy, "but he's in bad shape. He's on the floor, rolling around and moaning."

"Oh no!" I said. "We've got to get in there."

"There's a latch on the other side of the door," said Quincy. "But I can't lift it."

Gordon was inspecting the door frantically.

"Hey, look at this," he said, sticking his finger through a small hole in the door.

"It's not near the latch," Quincy said.

Gordon's brow furrowed. "Unless . . ." His eyes lit up. "Quincy, go get Medusa as fast as you can!"

"Aha!" Shane said, immediately realizing what Gordon meant to do.

Two minutes later, Medusa came down the stairs. She stood in front of the door, scratching her head.

"Which one of you is the longest?" she asked.

"I am," hissed one snake.

"No, it's ME," hissed another.

"I'm long enough," another said. "Let me try."

"Just hurry!" I yelled. "We're running out of time."

Medusa quickly put her head up against the door, and after a few more seconds of shoving and hissing, one snake went through quickly.

CLICK!

"Got it!" I yelled, pushing the door forward.

"Hey!" yelled Medusa, who was dragged forward with the door. "Give Jimmy a chance to slither back out of the hole!"

"Sorry!" I yelled. "The clock's ticking."

We rushed down a dark stone hallway and then popped out into a huge cave—with a rocket ship sitting in its center.

"Whoa!" I gasped.

"Awesome," said Shane.

"Why didn't you tell us the spaceship was in here, Quincy?" Gordon asked.

"You never asked," he replied.

I was stunned. It looked more like a funky skyscraper than a spaceship—all glass and metal.

"Look up there, you can see the stars," said Ben, pointing to a huge hole in the roof of the cave. Forest vegetation poured over the side.

"Look at the bottom set!" Nabila pointed at Frederick, slumped against the ship, motionless.

"Frederick. FREDERICK!"

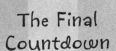

The Final Countdown

Shane rushed over to Frederick. "Are you okay?" he asked.

Frederick woke up from a daze and slowly got to his feet.

"Whew!" said Nabila.

"No, I'm fine," said the giant monster. "This is a safe place for me. This was my home when I was first created by my father. After the sangala attack, I decided to retreat here."

"Why were you moaning and rolling around?" asked Gordon.

Frederick stared up at the huge ship, a tear in his eye. "This wonderful monument makes me miss my father."

"It's all right," said Shane, patting Frederick on the back. "Let it out."

"NO!" I screeched. "Let it out later! We've got to go in five minutes, or we'll have to wait for weeks! Director Z might not even be alive then."

Frederick looked shocked, but he pulled himself together.

"Quincy, go get the other monsters," I said. "Tell them to get down here immediately. NOW!" I turned to Frederick. "How do we get into the ship?"

"Ship?" Frederick asked.

"Yes," Shane said, pointing up. "The rocket ship."

"You called it a monument," said Ben. "Don't you even know what it is?"

"My time here was short," said Frederick, "and I was confused in my first weeks. That's why I ran away from my father. Without thinking. By the time I remembered where he was, I couldn't get back. But I always had the image of this magnificent structure in my mind. I couldn't believe my luck when we moved here."

"Neither can we," I said. "That ship is going to take us to the moon, but we have to leave in the next four minutes. How do you open it?"

"How should I know?" Frederick said, frustrated.

"But you're the engine that powers it," said Gordon. "Maybe you have some special power to open the door."

"Don't worry about it," said Ben, standing at the

base of the rocket ship. "I think we just pull this lever."

He pulled the lever, and the stairway slowly came out of the bottom of the rocket, clinking and clanking.

With a great SCREEECH, it came to a stop . . . two feet above the ground.

"This thing is pretty old," said Nabila. "Are you sure we want to do this?"

"Yes, I'm sure," I said. "Now, where are those monsters? Frederick, come with me onto the ship. We've got to figure out how you power it up as soon as possible."

I helped him reach the first step, and then we both rushed up the stairs. As soon as Frederick was inside, small bulbs lit up. We could see more metal and glass.

"Where would the engine be?" I said.

We ran deeper into the ship, passing large mazes of crisscrossing pipes. I noticed that most of them led to the same place.

"Let's go that way," I yelled, and we turned down a tight hallway, filled mostly with the pipes, that led to . . .

"The engine room!" I yelled.

Insanely large generators lined the walls, and in the center, surrounded by glass, was a metal chair with a metal helmet hanging above. It looked ominously like an electric chair.

"I think you're supposed to sit there," I said to Frederick. "Get strapped in, quick! We've only got three minutes."

Frederick sat down in the chair, and the metal helmet lowered onto his head.

CRACK. SNAP. SNIP! CRACK!

Lightning shot through Frederick, leaving dark marks on the glass.

Now I know why that glass is there, I thought.

The lightning got stronger, and Frederick spasmed in the chair.

"YARRRRGGGGHHH!" he screamed, shaking and sputtering.

"Frederick, are you okay?" I yelled over the cracks.

"This is amazing!" said Frederick. "Finally, something that utilizes all of my energies! It's absolutely thrilling."

His body shook, and the lights on the ship glowed brighter. The generators hummed softly.

"I'm running to get the others," I yelled. "Keep it going!"

I jumped down the stairs of the rocket, forgetting the last step was two feet off the ground. I fell, but caught myself and rolled. I stood up to find all of the monsters there.

"ALL RIGHT!" I yelled. "There's a cargo hold in the second level—everyone pack in!"

"There's no way I'm going into space," cackled one of the witches.

"We've just recovered from a major attack," added Roy.

Half the crowd erupted in protest.

"What are you going to do?" yelled Shane over the crowd—and the growing hum of the rocket ship.

I reached in my pocket and felt the bloodstone there. I could feel its power as I rubbed it.

"QUIET!" I yelled.

The monsters were quiet, but I still needed to yell over the roar of the engine.

"Director Z needs our help. ALL of our help. We've got two minutes to get on the ship. Let's get going. I COMMAND IT!"

That was all it took. The monsters rushed aboard, the stronger ones helping the older ones onto the busted staircase.

"Gordon and Ben," I said. "Stay with the monsters and get them into the cargo hold. Shane and Nabila, we've got to find the bridge."

Between the roar of the engine and the screams of the monsters, my head spun. There was only one place I hadn't seen on the ship, so I ran there, my friends following.

"Here it is!" I said, bursting onto the bridge.

"It looks like the bridge of an ocean liner," said Shane.

The room was filled with levers and switches, and in the center was the biggest lever of them all, next to the ship's wheel. It was labeled QUARTER THRUST, HALF THRUST, and FULL THRUST.

"But how do we start it?" I asked.

"Wait, over here!" Nabila said. She pointed at a huge red button. "This has to be it."

"Unless it's the self-destruct button," said Shane.

"No time," I said, leaning forward and pushing the red button.

The whole ship shook violently, rattling our teeth.

"Guys," yelled Ben as he came in. "There wasn't enough room! We're all on, but not everyone fit into the cargo hold."

Twenty old monsters came in after him, crowding the already-small bridge. Two zombies blocked the massive lever in the center.

"Move to the side, guys," I said, and pulled the lever as far as I could. "I can only get it to half thrust!"

The stronger monsters pushed through the small crowd that had formed on the deck to help. Grigore, who still had real teeth and black hair, jumped forward and pushed down . . .

CLICK.

The lever was now at full thrust, and the ship began shaking even harder.

Nuts and bolts flew down from the ceiling.

"There's got to be something that starts the liftoff sequence," I yelled. "Shane, try that lever."

Shane pulled a lever. NOTHING.

Nabila pulled another lever.

A metal panel exploded from the wall, showering sparks over Howie the werewolf. His hairy neck caught on fire. Shane jumped on him to put it out, while Roy, trying hard not to singe his fur, put the panel back in place.

"Look!" yelled a witch.

She pointed at a small clock on a panel on the right side of the bridge.

It was at T-minus fifteen seconds and counting.

"Okay, hold on, everyone!" I roared, and grabbed the wheel.

Ten seconds.

The ship sounded like it was falling apart. I could hear Frederick screaming.

Five seconds.

A crack formed in the glass in front of us.

"Wa-hoooooo!" hooted Shane.

Three seconds.

Two . . .

One . . .

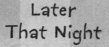

Later That Night

"Hello? Helllooooo?!"

Chris's mother knocked furiously at the front door of Gallow Manor.

"Open this door this instant!" she insisted. "I know that you're in there, Chris! Shane!"

She paused for a minute, and a worried look washed over her face.

"I hope you're in there!" she said. "It's so late! You should have been home hours ago."

The headlights of a car flashed into her face, as it came up the road. It stopped in front of her, and the principal of Rio Vista Middle School stepped out of the driver's seat.

"Thank goodness you're here," said Chris's mother. "I couldn't think of who else to reach out to. I wasn't ready to call the police and make a fuss . . . not yet!"

"I'm sorry I'm so late," said Principal Prouty. "I volunteer at the animal shelter after school, and we've been having a problem with overpopulation. And my allergies have been terrible. What seems to be the matter here? Surely somebody must be home?"

"No, and I've been knocking for the last half hour," she shrieked.

The door slowly creaked open. She and the principal looked at each other.

They both headed to the entryway, but were pushed back by a ghostly old figure in what appeared to be a naval officer's uniform. He glowed strangely in the moonlight.

"Why are you at my door?" asked the old man.

"I demand to speak to Director Zachary!" Chris's mother screeched. "Or a nurse. Or anyone! Where is Chris Taylor?"

"They've all left," said the mysterious old figure.

"All of them?" asked the principal.

"What do you mean, 'they've all left'?" asked Chris's mother.

"I mean exactly what I said!" hissed the old man. "Nobody's home. They're all gone. And I have no idea when they'll be back. Satisfied?"

The door slammed in their faces.

"How could they all be gone?" asked the principal. She looked confused and sad. "We've got to find them. Right away."

"Your concern for your students is touching," said Chris's mother.

"It's not just the students I'm worried about," said the principal.

Chris's mother gave her a questioning look.

"I'm also worried about my grandfather."

About the author . . .

M. D. Payne is a mad scientist who creates monsters by stitching together words instead of dead body parts. After nearly a decade in multimedia production for public radio, he entered children's publishing as a copywriter and marketer. Monster Juice is his debut series. He lives in the tiny village of New York City with his wife and baby girl, and hopes to add a hairy, four-legged monster to his family soon.